This book must be returned by the date specified at the time of issue as
the DATE DUE FOR RETURN.
The loan may be extended (personally, by post, telephone or online) for
a further period if the book is not required by another reader, by quoting
the above number / author / title.

Enquiries: 01709 336774

www.rotherham.gov.uk/libraries

THE ASH MURDERS &
OTHER STORIES

An apparent case of spontaneous human combustion is enough to test the very limits of Detective Inspector Dryer's beliefs, so when Augustus Smith appears, claiming that the victim was targeted by an ancient demon and that others will suffer the same fate, this proves too much to take. But could Smith possibly be telling the truth . . . ? This and four other tales of the strange and mysterious make up this collection from Edmund Glasby.

EDMUND GLASBY

THE ASH MURDERS & OTHER STORIES

Complete and Unabridged

LINFORD
Leicester

First published in Great Britain

First Linford Edition
published 2014

Copyright © 2013 by Edmund Glasby

A catalogue record for this book is available
from the British Library.

ISBN 978–1–4448–1869–7

Published by
F. A. Thorpe (Publishing)
Anstey, Leicestershire

Set by Words & Graphics Ltd.
Anstey, Leicestershire
Printed and bound in Great Britain by
T. J. International Ltd., Padstow, Cornwall

This book is printed on acid-free paper

1

THE ASH MURDERS

*Was it an accident, murder
or something else . . . ?*

Detective Inspector John Dryer took a cigarette from the packet he kept inside his raincoat pocket. Cupping the struck match against the wind, he lit it and took a deep drag, eyes narrowing as he stared at Martin Stevens, the forensic scientist, who stood before him. There was an unmistakable look of confusion on the other's face that he had never seen before throughout their fifteen years or so of working together. He flicked the spent match away.

'As I said on the phone, John, this one's got me beaten.' Stevens shook his head, one hand resting atop the chest-high, railed metal gate that gave access to the park. Beyond the gate was a narrow lane that ran for perhaps a hundred yards before disappearing into the shadowy tunnel under the railway bridge. Halfway along the path, close to a park bench, stood a police officer, looking down at something that lay heaped on the ground. The crime scene photographer was now packing up his equipment, getting ready to leave.

Dryer took the cigarette from his mouth and blew out a cloud of smoke. 'Beaten? In what way?'

Stevens paused for a moment, framing his response. He coughed slightly. 'Well, let's just say you can forget about doing a chalk outline.' He held the gate open. 'This is what I refer to as a dustpan and brush job. Come, take a look for yourself.'

Dryer suddenly felt a chill sensation run through him. Whether it was due to the late autumnal wind that suddenly grew more intense, gusting through the elms and the oaks that stood nearby, he didn't know, but it carried with it a strong sense of foreboding. Walking that short stretch of pathway towards where the victim lay filled him with a growing sense of dread, something he had never experienced before. Sure, there had been times when he had seen things that were truly gruesome, things which most people were mercifully unaware of, but for some reason the prospect of what he was going to see had him on edge. There was a sudden thickness in his throat. He now realised that the heap on the ground, which, from a distance, he had taken to be nothing more than a pile of windblown leaves, was smoking. Wisps of grey spiralled and billowed in the wind, carrying with it a most horrendous stench. Face contorting in disgust, he moved closer, wincing further as he made out the charred bones. The worst sight, however, was the relatively unscathed head, which lay close to the park bench. Shaking his head in disbelief, he grimaced upon seeing an overly curious squirrel scamper forward to have a better look.

The police officer noticed it and shooed it away.

'Well as you can see, aside from the head, most of the remains are, by and large, incinerated. Virtually carbonised. The undertaker won't know whether to order a coffin or an urn.' Stevens reached into a pocket and took out a small plastic specimen bag. 'A proper examination will have to wait till after we get the remains to the laboratory but sifting through the topmost layer of ash I found this.' He handed the bag to Dryer. 'I believe it to be a surgical implant of some kind. It's very badly melted, but it's my guess that it's a knee or hip joint replacement. Further examination should verify this one way or another.'

Dryer briefly studied the blackened item in the bag before handing it back. 'What in God's name happened?'

'Well, as I told you on the phone, I've no definite explanation. However, whatever fire caused this must have been extremely intense, for bone doesn't burn like that. It just dries out and shatters, unless subjected to temperatures in excess of fifteen hundred degrees Fahrenheit, the kind of temperatures reached in an industrial oven or a crematorium. In addition, and this is perhaps more surprising, the fire appears to have been extremely localised, as evident from the fact that a completely unscathed newspaper was found close by. Less than two feet away. I'd say we're looking at either a freakish lightning strike or . . . an occurrence of spontaneous human combustion. The sole witness account that we have would seem to suggest something of this order.'

'Who is the witness, and where?' Dryer's questions were directed to the police officer.

'A Mr. Peter Laynham, sir. He's been admitted to St. Catherine's Hospital,' answered the man. 'Extreme shock, I believe. He was half-mad, ranting almost. Some of the things he was saying were more than a little . . . outlandish, shall we say.'

'*Outlandish?*'

'Why yes, sir.' The officer reached into his pocket and removed a notebook. He flipped it open. 'Understandably, it was hard getting much from Mr. Laynham but apparently about seven o'clock this morning he had been out jogging, when he saw a dark-suited gentlemen sat on the bench in front of him. He had come from the direction of the tunnel over there and believed he heard the man talking rather loudly although there was no one else visible. He said that the words were foreign, certainly not English. Then, while he was still some distance away, the man got suddenly to his feet and started to flail his arms around wildly as though he was being harangued by a swarm of wasps or something. According to Mr. Laynham . . . the man's head then fell off and, suddenly, he was ablaze, a human torch. And, well — ' He finished by just looking down and gesturing, rather hopelessly, to the smouldering heap.

Dryer took a few steps and bent down in order to examine the blood-spattered head. It was that of a man; dark black hair ruffled and streaked through with shades of light grey. Age-wise, he was probably in his mid-fifties. There was an Middle Eastern look to his olive-tanned features; almond-shaped brown eyes glared wildly with horror from behind the cracked lenses of a delicately framed pair of bent spectacles. For some macabre reason he suddenly remembered something he had once read — an article about those aristocratic French unfortunates who had been guillotined — about how the brain was supposed to still function for several seconds after decapitation enabling one to witness the aftermath of one's own beheading. The very thought made him shiver.

'Although it doesn't quite fit in with the witness report, which, to be honest, I think we have to treat with some level of scepticism, I think the best possible explanation is, as I said earlier, spontaneous human combustion,' suggested Stevens.

Dryer stood up and turned to the forensic scientist. 'What exactly is that? I mean, I've heard of it, but I've always thought that it was just one of those weird phenomena. Like that other thing whereby people claim to have bled from their palms and feet as though crucified.'

'That's stigmata.' Stevens shook his head. 'No. This is something entirely different. Had you asked me before this morning whether I believed the human body could just suddenly burst into flames without a source of ignition I'd have laughed at the very concept. However, I just can't see how else this could have happened. There have been numerous reports of this kind of thing occurring but they always end up in the weird magazines, you know, the sort of fringe, paranormal stuff. That said, I do recollect reading a few years back an article in one of the more credible scientific publications detailing a supposed outbreak of S.H.C. in America in which over thirty individuals were all burnt in a similar manner to what we have here. However, in virtually all of those cases the remains were always found close to an ignition source; an electric fire, a television set, a hairdryer, overhead electricity cables or some such. Clearly, in this case, there is no such thing which just makes it all the more baffling.'

'And the head? How do you explain that? It looks to me as though that's been sliced off, by a sword or an axe.'

'I agree.' Stevens rubbed his chin thoughtfully. 'That's even more difficult to explain. Certainly in the cases of spontaneous human combustion I've read about the extremities were quite often found relatively intact. What I mean is; legs and arms were often found whole, untouched almost, amidst the ashes. It's almost as though an intense heat consumed the torso and engulfed that alone, extinguishing itself once the core of the body was destroyed, causing the limbs to just 'cave-in' as it were. Obviously in this instance it would appear that — '

'Hang on, wait a minute,' interrupted Dryer. 'The witness states that the head was removed prior to the body setting alight.'

'Witness confusion. It has to be. The man was clearly shocked at what he saw. I mean, let's face it, spontaneous human combustion is hard enough to believe, but people's heads just falling off?'

'Can we be sure that they're linked? Can we take it as a given that the head and the burnt remains belong to the same individual?'

Stevens' look of puzzlement grew. 'Lab tests should be able to confirm that. But have you got any reason to suspect otherwise?'

'No, but we have to be certain. At the moment I don't know what we have here. Is it a dreadful accident, even though I don't see how it could possibly have happened? Murder? Again, equally mysterious unless the witness is in fact the perpetrator. Or is it . . . I don't know, a natural occurrence? Could this be something attributable to heavy smoking or excessive alcohol intake?'

'Smoking, maybe. Although I don't know how. I suppose a lit cigarette, falling inside an inner article of clothing . . . ' Stevens knew that his explanation was far-fetched, almost to the point of ridicule, but he was truly confused. There weren't that many more straws for him to grasp at.

Dryer's own cigarette had burnt low now. He removed it from his mouth, looked at it strangely, threw it to one side, walked over and crushed it underfoot.

★ ★ ★

It was mid-afternoon and Dryer was now sat at the desk in his office going through some of his paperwork. There was still no definite identification of the victim despite the fact that he had a team working on the case. That the head had been preserved offered a good chance that sooner, rather than later, he would be able to put a name to the unfortunate so that, at the very least, next of kin could be informed of the tragedy. He himself now believed it to have been a natural occurrence, no matter how unlikely that hypothesis seemed. The more he had listened to Stevens' notion of spontaneous human combustion, the more he had gradually come round to that theory. After all, if it was murder, then how in hell's name had it been executed without a single trace of flammable material present?

The remains were now in the morgue, no doubt being sifted through by the forensic expert. If he turned up anything then it might alter the nature of the case but so far he had heard nothing.

He had been in two minds about going out to St. Catherine's in order to see if it was possible to question the witness, Mr.

Laynham, but had decided against it. Again, if new evidence arose to suggest foul play then that was an avenue of enquiry he could pursue at a later date.

There came a firm knock on his door.

'Come in.'

The door was opened by one of his officers. 'Sir, there's a man here to see you. He says it's vitally important and that it's to do with the discovery this morning.'

'That's good. Send him in.'

'Yes sir. I'll get him.' The officer turned and went back to the main desk. He returned moments later with a tall, straight-backed, well-dressed man who looked to be in his early sixties. There was an air of distinguished erudition in the stranger's bright blue eyes. His hair was a startling white and he had a well-groomed goatee.

Dryer waited in silence as his visitor entered and took a seat opposite.

The door closed as the officer left.

'I understand you have some information for us.' It wasn't so much a question as a statement of fact.

'Yes, I believe I do. Allow me introduce myself. My name is Augustus Smith. I'm a collector of Middle Eastern antiquities. I have a boutique here in the city.'

'I see, well Mr. Smith anything you can give me to help clear up this unfortunate incident will be extremely welcome. Can I ask, did you know the deceased? And secondly, just how do you know about this as there has been no news released about it as far as I'm aware?'

'I'll answer your second question first if I may. I arrived at the park shortly after you left and spoke with the policeman on duty just as to what had happened. He told me readily enough once I explained that I was concerned over the welfare of a friend of mine. Although he didn't provide me with the details, I . . . I've seen enough to know what to expect.'

'I'm confused. *'To know what to expect'?* Just what do you mean by that?' Dryer sat up in his chair, his eyes boring into the other. Was this man somehow linked to the terrible happening this morning? Criminologists had a theory that the perpetrator of a crime was often compelled to return to the scene. Like a dog to its vomit, he thought.

'I think you'll just have to believe me when I tell you that I've seen this thing before.'

Dryer tilted his head slightly. 'Seen what exactly?'

Smith paused for a moment, clearly unsure as to how to continue. 'The body . . . I take it was terribly burnt? Beyond all recognition, save for the head?'

'That information hasn't been disclosed as yet. Just how do you know this?' Dryer's suspicion rocketed. Unless this enigmatic stranger had been the actual murderer or another witness who had not come forward at the time surely there was no way he could — or rather should — be privy to this information. Surely his officers at the scene wouldn't have been forthcoming with such sensitive details. That went beyond all protocols of police investigation.

'As I told you, Inspector, I've seen this thing before.'

'Where?' Dryer leant his elbows on the desk and interlinked his fingers, not taking his stern gaze from the informant.

'Baghdad. Mosul. Tikrit. And in half a dozen other towns and cities throughout Iraq. And now, it would appear, it's here, in England.'

'I'm lost. Just what do you mean?'

'Can I ask, Inspector, are you a religious man?'

'Can't say that I am. What's that got to do with anything?' Dryer responded sharply. He was fast beginning to lose his patience. He had hoped for something a bit more relevant than this seemingly useless load of nonsense.

'Well then, you're going to find it hard to accept what I'm about to tell you. You see — '

There came another knock at the door but this time the person on the other side didn't wait for a reply, merely barging straight in.

It was Stevens. His look of unsuccessfully suppressed excitement turned instantly to one of surprise upon seeing Dryer's visitor.

'Have you got anything for me?' Dryer asked.

'Yes, but — ' The forensic scientist threw a swift glance at Smith. It was abundantly clear he didn't want to continue in the presence of the other.

Dryer nodded. 'Mr Smith. I'd appreciate it if you'd please step outside for a minute or two whilst I have a word with my colleague.'

With a slight nod of acquiescence, Smith rose from his chair and went outside.

Stevens closed the door behind him. 'Who's that?' he asked.

'Mr. Augustus Smith. He seems to know something about what happened in the park although I'm not exactly sure what to make of him. That he knows something is pretty apparent but exactly what, I don't know as yet, nor his level of direct involvement. He claims to have seen things like this before, in Iraq of all places.' Dryer stopped, noticing a sudden strange look on Stevens' face.

'*Iraq?* Are you sure?'

'Yes, why? Are you alright?'

Stevens sat down. 'Hmm. Well there's a coincidence.'

'Is this something to do with your

laboratory findings?'

'Forensically, everything was as one would expect. The head was that of a Middle Eastern male in his mid-fifties. There was a touch of glaucoma in his left eye and I've been unable to match the spectacles to any local opticians, giving weight to the possibility that he is relatively new to this area if not this country. His teeth weren't in that great a condition either. However, that molten nugget that I originally took for some kind of surgical implant was nothing of the kind. I couldn't have been further from the mark. Under the microscope, I found out that it was in fact a piece of partially molten bronze and that it had been a small figurine of sorts. I've been late in getting back to you because I ran it by a friend of mine at the Museum and within a couple of hours she got back to me telling me that, as far as she could make out, it was a representation of the Babylonian Daemon-God, Pazuzu.'

There was a certain level of indignation in Dryer's cough as he shifted in his seat. He threw a surreptitious glance at the wall clock and it was clear that, for him at least, this day had gone on far too long. 'So, we've got an ancient demon on the loose, have we? My, the Chief Superintendent's going to love hearing about that!'

Stevens chuckled, but it was far from a genuine show of mirth. 'Is that what he's been on about?' He flicked his head to indicate the man waiting outside.

'Get him back in. See if he can shed any more light on this. I still don't have a name as yet.'

Stevens nodded, opened the office door and re-admitted Smith.

'You said you knew the victim. A name, if you please.' It wasn't quite Dryer's normal interrogation tone of voice that he reserved for the hard cases, but it soon could be.

'I believe the deceased to be Mr. Ali Hassan Jamal, an Iraqi national who travelled to England in order to seek my assistance. Alas, I was too late.'

'Your assistance. How exactly?'

'I possess certain . . . powers. Powers that can be used to keep certain things at bay.'

18

Dryer and Stevens exchanged bemused, knowing glances. They clearly had a deranged individual on their hands. It wouldn't have been the first time such idiots had clouded cases with their bizarre claims and admissions.

'I don't expect you to believe me, however I will leave you with this warning. I fully expect something identical to happen again quite soon. Unfortunately there will be others like Mr. Jamal, of that I am certain. Others will share a similar fate. This will only come to a conclusion when the evil entity that is doing this is defeated. And when I say defeated, I mean killed.'

'I'd be rather careful of what I said if I were you, Mr. Smith. Apart from the obvious nonsense, making threats like that could land you in serious trouble. You talk about possessing powers to keep things at bay. Well I possess certain powers to keep people like yourself out of harm's reach. Just what is it you're on about?' There was an intense seriousness in Dryer's tone despite the fact that he was certain that Smith was more than a touch unbalanced. He had to be. What other explanation for all of this talk so far could there be? All of this veiled insinuation about demons and evil entities . . .

'Some thirty years ago, I worked as an archaeologist out in Iraq. I was an assistant field director under Sir Leonard Woolley, working at the ancient Sumerian city of Ur. Early one morning, several weeks into our excavations, one of the Arab labourers failed to turn up for work. It wasn't that unheard of or that surprising, however, news soon hit our camp that a terrible 'accident' had happened in one of the settlements nearby. A man's severed head had been discovered atop a heap of charred bone and ash in one of the side streets not far from the marketplace. I found out later that the man had been the missing labourer and — '

'Mr. Smith. I've got no time for this. Now, if you've got anything useful to say would you please get on with it,' Dryer interrupted impatiently.

'It's clear you haven't the time to hear my story so I guess I'd better just cut to the chase, as it were. Basically, Inspector, what we have here is a vengeful demon, an *efreeti*, to give it its proper name, which has been loosened to wreak vengeance on certain individuals by Pazuzu. The first victim, the unfortunate from the archaeological dig had found a votive cache of bronze heads of the Daemon God, perhaps over a hundred of them and made off. No doubt he sought to sell them on the sly. Such criminality was rife. Regardless, those who are in possession of them are all either dead or in grave danger. As you have discovered, the unfortunate Mr. Jamal had one such relic. I too, have one.' Smith reached into a jacket pocket and removed a small, roughly spherical shaped lump of carved bronze. He extended his arm, held it out on his upturned palm. 'I wouldn't touch it if I were you. The sorcery that was contained in the one you discovered has been spent. It is no longer dangerous. This however still retains its potency.'

Dryer edged over the desk in order to get a better look. There was a violent, blood-thirsty, carnivorous glare in the bulging eyes and the snarling, dog-like face that spoke of chaos and depravity; hatred and malevolence. Despite the fact that he could have ordered the other to hand it over there was something about it that urged him not to. It seemed to radiate evil and danger.

'You say that everyone who has one of these is in danger,' commented Stevens. 'I take it that includes you.'

Smith loosened his cravat and unbuttoned the collar of his shirt. From beneath, he removed a length of chain from which dangled a circular medallion. 'This is the Seal of Solomon. It keeps me protected from the powers of the efreeti. Provided I wear it at all times, I am safe.'

'Do you honestly expect us to believe any of this Arabian Nights nonsense? Efreetis? Magic amulets? Come on, this is absolute rubbish,' Dryer argued volubly. 'You'll be telling us next that it flies around on a magic carpet.'

'I can assure you, Inspector, that it's all very real. Whether you believe me or not is of course your decision, but I can assure you that there will be further victims.'

* * *

Smith was correct with his terrifying prediction, for three days later, Dryer found himself staring down at the smouldering, fire-blackened remains of another victim. This time, however, the individual was readily identified as librarian and scholar, Doctor Jack Bentley. Once again, the detached head was found nearby, close to the row of bookshelves at which it was assumed, he had been working when tragedy struck. The fact that truly baffled Dryer was that, despite the obvious ferocity of the fire which must have been severe — intense enough to reduce a man to nothing more than a heap of bone and ash — there was little or no damage to the immediate surroundings.

The whole library should have gone up like a tinderbox.

Stevens shook his head in disbelief as he emerged from behind one of the rows of books. 'This is absolutely unreal. There's no sign of intrusion and once again no presence of flammable material.

Really, John, I've got no idea how this happened. According to Miss Fowler who had found the 'body" Doctor Bentley was working late last night, going through some of the catalogues and rearranging the books. He was alone from six o'clock when she left.'

The smell was dreadful, repellent, eye-watering. It reminded Dryer of the time he had almost set his kitchen ablaze after forgetting about the rashers of bacon he had been grilling for breakfast. It had taken two days to remove the offensive smell even after opening all of the windows to ensure maximum ventilation. At least the first burnt remains had been discovered out in the open, but here —

For some macabre reason he felt as though his eyes were being constantly drawn to the severed head. 'That look on his face,' he commented. 'It's as though he was witness to something absolutely horrendous.'

'I agree.' Stevens knelt down and put on his surgical gloves. Gingerly, he lifted the head, scrutinising the grisly piece of evidence. 'Just like the other one. There's

24

no sign of cauterization leading me to the fairly confident conclusion that it was removed prior to the actual fire by means of a sharp-bladed implement.'

'You mean he was decapitated. Then set alight?'

'I'm pretty sure of it.'

'But how? Why? And you realise that we're now looking at murder?'

'It would appear so.' Stevens began delicately sifting through the ashes. 'And Laynham's still in hospital so he's out of the frame.'

'Right. Time to pay that oddball Smith a visit. I've had a feeling about him — '

'Here we are.' Stevens retrieved something from the smouldering pile.

'What is it?' There was a faint trace of reluctance in Dryer's question; a quavering in his voice indicative of his concern. It was as though he dreaded hearing the answer.

'If I'm not mistaken I'd say it's one of those bronze heads.'

* * *

It was late afternoon when Dryer drove out to Smith's house and the light was already fading from the sky. This part of town was not well known to him and he looked in admiration at the large, handsome houses on either side of the road. There were some pleasing Georgian buildings with what he always thought of as 'open features'; warm, welcoming kinds of homes. Driving further along the street, checking the numbers as he went, he was a little disappointed as the style of architecture changed to Victorian. The simple, rectangular windows replaced by pointed gables and slightly mediaeval-looking decoration. Number twenty-three which appeared on his right hand was another Victorian Gothic edifice with a high wall and an iron gate. He parked his car and got out, pulling his coat tighter to stave off the chill air. Pushing open the gate, he then strode briskly to the front door, noticing that Smith must own the whole house for there was no evidence of it having been divided into flats as so many of these larger houses commonly were.

The curiously wrought iron door knocker was fashioned in the shape of a grotesque half-man, half-bull hybrid with bizarre curly hair and Dryer hesitated for a moment before using it. Three dull echoes chased themselves along the hallway beyond and yet, surprisingly, made comparatively little exterior sound as though strangely muffled.

The best part of a minute passed and he was about to knock once more when he heard the rattle of several security chains and then the door opened the narrowest of cracks.

'Yes?' The voice was weird, alien almost.

That single word, that one question, prompted Dryer to take a couple of steps back. He could see little of the individual beyond but he got the impression that the other was tall and somehow intimidating. Was it just his imagination or did he see a neon flash of violet in the shadows beyond.

'I — I've come to see Mr Smith. Is he — is he in?' An inner voice was calling out to Dryer to leave this place whilst he had the chance. To get away, whilst his mind and body remained intact. There was strangeness here; a conclusion he had reached within two minutes of standing on the doorstep. How much worse were things going to be inside?

'Yes.' There was no alteration in the voice at all. No change in tone or inflection and yet that one word response seemed to imply something far greater than a mere affirmation.

Dryer was uncomfortable with the current situation. He felt awkward, not knowing how to initiate any form of further dialogue. Mustering his courage, he stepped forward, instilling some level of authority back into his manner. 'If Mr. Smith is in it's important that I speak to him. This is official police business. I must ask that you step aside and admit me entrance.'

In utter silence the door swung open, permitting Dryer to enter.

It was dim and shadowy, and yet Dryer did a double take upon making out the other's admittedly tenebrous dimensions. He must have stood over seven, perhaps eight feet in height and he was as slim as a beanpole. Eyeing the lanky giant suspiciously, he gulped and strode inside. No sooner had he crossed the threshold and taken a few short steps into the hall than the door swung shut behind him.

Sudden luminosity brightened the long, narrow room as two chandeliers flared into light.

Dryer's heart leapt into his mouth as he noticed that he was alone. There was no sign of the weird being that had opened the door, nor was there anywhere he could have gone, unless he had somehow managed to slip outside even as he had come inside. That explanation seemed impossible however considering the size of the individual. A small, fleet-footed child might have been able to pull off such a dextrous feat but —

Even as he stared, perplexed, bewildered, his eyes blinking unbelievingly, Dryer heard a muffled, dull-sounding explosion come from somewhere almost directly overhead. There then came a shout, followed by a second bang somewhat louder than the first. The lights shook and flickered for a moment.

'What the hell!?' Dryer cursed savagely and stared with some alarm at the ceiling, half-expecting it to come crashing down in a cave-in of beams and plaster. Fear rooted him to the spot for several heartbeats and there was a tingling in his spine that felt as though a trickle of ice was beginning to slowly seep down his back. He was about to spin round and open the front door — assuming that it had not been mysteriously locked — in order to escape, when he saw Smith appear at the top of the staircase at the end of the hall.

'Inspector. If you'd be so good as to get up here as quickly as — '

Before Smith could finish, the front door, now at Dryer's back, juddered fiercely. It was as though something powerful had taken hold of the entire frame and had given it a good shake. The locks rattled like a violent lunatic in chains.

'Quick! Upstairs!' shouted Smith.

Uncertain as to what was happening, Dryer took a couple of staggering steps, his eyes now on the front door. With utter horror, he began to see the interior wooden surface begin to blacken; smoking, scorched holes now appearing as though it had been struck by the intense rays of the sun which had been focused and magnified through a strong lens. The smell of burning wood struck his nostrils. Then came a bellowing cry and for some inexplicable reason, Dryer had the image of the fiendish door-knocker coming to life and uttering that unearthly noise.

'I would be quick if I were you, Inspector. My *lamassu* door guardian won't hold the efreeti for long.'

The front door was now beginning to char and warp; buckle inwards. Tendrils of black, lachrymatory smoke began to fill the entryway and Dryer, fully realising that escape that way was no longer an option, made a run for the stairs. He was halfway up when he heard another snort of pain and anger. And then, with an almighty crash, the door smashed open in fragments of fiery wood. Flaming pieces landed like burning kindling on the carpet.

Somewhere at the edge of his vision, he saw the hall brighten, come afire with a burst of blazing colours. His eyes twisted horribly as they tried to bring whatever it was into sharper focus. They failed dismally every time. It was as if he was looking at everything that was happening through a twisted red haze that blurred his vision, making it impossible for him to see properly. Then, abruptly, the red haze was gone. There was a riotous clashing of colours in the middle of the hall. A chaotic madness of reds and yellows that was horrible to see and he felt terror begin its slow seep against his sanity. In those brief seconds, strange, hideous, distorted shapes flitted amidst the wavering background of heatless flame. At any moment, he expected something grimacing and terrible to surge up at him from that illusionary conflagration, clawing for his body; something that didn't have a human face at all, and stared at him out of black, soulless, unblinking eyes; fixing him with an evil, malignant stare.

'Quick! Everyone into the circle.' Smith all but pushed Dryer into a large room at the top of the landing.

With only seconds to realise what was happening and take in his surroundings, Dryer realised that there were two other individuals present as well as Smith. One of them was the giant, ectomorphic being who had answered the door whilst the other was a fair-haired man in his fifties. The man was smartly dressed and normal-looking, except for the fear and terror in his face, discernible in the manner in which he stared wildly all around him, but it was the giant —

Smith suddenly slammed shut the door of the room and forcibly steered Dryer into the centre of the room where the others were gathered.

A storm of unreality battered at Dryer as he tried to mentally process everything that was unfolding. His eyes were drawn again to the bizarre being that had opened the front door before vanishing. The man — if indeed it were such — had a pale golden-blue colour to his flesh, which glistened and scintillated as though it had been sprinkled with a strange, exotic confetti. The being's head was disproportionately large in relation to its tall, thin body, like that of a hydrocephalic and the eyes were a peculiar violet colour; the face — grim and unsmiling. What clothing it wore was similarly peculiar, unlike anything he had ever seen before, alien almost.

'There's little time for an explanation, Inspector. Stay within the circle.'

Looking to the floor, Dryer saw that the four of them were all stood within a large circle that had been drawn with a range of coloured chalks. There were curious, cabbalistic symbols that ran in a ring around the circumference, all of which meant absolutely nothing to him whatsoever although he suspected they must have been linked to some form of Black Magic. What other explanation was there for this unholy experience? He was about to say something when the door swung open.

In the doorway stood a dark-suited, bald, fat man, his fleshy, heavily-jowled face awash with sweat and pure malice. There was a something in his piggy, narrow-set eyes that gave them a strong hint of unconstrained anger and malice as though he bore a deep-rooted hatred of all bar himself.

Smith took a forward step, still remaining well within the circle. 'Klaus Weidenreich. I should have known.'

'Augustus, my old friend.' Weidenreich's voice was slick and oily and undoubtedly German. His eyes were dark and dangerous, like tar pits into which the unwary could become stuck; drown in their terrible depths. 'You know why I'm here, Smith. There are only two of my Lord Pazuzu's tokens remaining. You have one . . . and Doctor Harris,' he nodded to the fair-haired man, 'has the other.'

Dryer was finding it hard to retain a grip on himself in the face of this insanity. Things were happening which he had never, even in his wildest nightmares, considered possible. With some level of mental resignation, he knew that all of his hard-nosed police training and experience was of little use in a situation such as this. He had no authority here — a realisation that only increased the fear and the mind-numbing terror which now ran, virtually unchecked through the very core of his being. Tough talking and the threat of a jail sentence was of no use here. Admittedly, a gun may have been useful, but somehow he even doubted that.

Weidenreich looked down with a derisive sneer at the drawn circle. 'How long do you think your pathetic protection will keep you safe? An hour, maybe two? And as for your *djinn* . . . well we both know it will be no match against the efreeti. As to your third 'friend', with him I have no grievance.' He stared directly at Dryer. 'So he may leave — ' Raising his right hand, he made a beckoning motion with it.

Instantly, Dryer felt much of the stiffness leave his body. And yet the sensation he experienced was as though he was no longer in control of his own muscles. His legs began walking of their own volition, and he was just about to cross over the circle when Smith cried out something in a language he had never heard before and he was brought to a complete standstill. A second later, he snapped out of the strange trance he had been put under and a firm resolution, hard as steel, returned to his mind. Under different circumstances, this would have been the time to strike back at the other, verbally if not physically. This, however, was not the time or the situation. Since stepping into this strange house and becoming embroiled in all of this devilry and occult malignancy, all vestiges of his sane, rational thought processes had dissipated, evaporated almost to the point of nothingness. All of his life he had prized himself on his no-nonsense approach to life, managing to maintain his mental well-being and outlook.

Weidenreich's look of disappointment at not having charmed Dryer into stepping outside the circle suddenly changed to one of surprise as Harris pulled a revolver from his jacket pocket. Next came the loud report as a bullet was fired, followed in rapid succession by five others. All but one hit their target and the room darkened as the bald-headed German sorcerer was sent flying, blood streaming from five bullet wounds.

Dryer's first reaction was one of shock. He was a Detective Inspector and someone had committed murder in the first degree right in front of his very eyes. However, the spectacle was made worse when, emitting a horrible, mocking laugh, Weidenreich began to get to his feet.

That dark wave of disbelief and horror surged at Dryer like a black tide once more. One bullet, certainly fired from that range and with that accuracy should have been enough to kill, but how on earth could someone survive getting hit by five? His mind was screaming silently as he noticed that two of the shots had left terrible gaping, bloody holes in Weidenreich's head. And yet, even now those wounds were closing, shrinking until they vanished completely. There was no longer any sign of blood. It was as though he had never been shot at all!

'He's the efreeti!' Smith shouted. 'It must have possessed him and taken his body. Devoured his very soul.'

The thing that had gone by the name of Klaus Weidenreich gave an unspeakably fiendish grin, baring a mouthful of jagged, shark-like teeth. Howling its fury, it then began to transform further, tearing its way out of the corpulent body with the razor sharp talons that had sprouted on the end of its fingers. Long, elastic strands of flesh stretched and snapped like lengths of rubber as a hideous entity began to reveal itself in its true, abominable form.

Dryer's nerve faltered and his mouth trembled as he tried to scream, to give some expression to the revulsion and the terror that threatened to rend him asunder as assuredly as the thing that now snarled before them intended on doing. Harris stumbled to his knees and covered his eyes, his ineffectual revolver falling from his quaking grasp. Smith too seemed to recoil, raising his arm in order to remove the talisman — The Seal of Solomon — that hung around his neck. The efreeti was a nightmare born of evil and chaos; a fire-loving, demonic elemental being whose sole purpose was to kill those who opposed it. Naked, its appearance was vaguely humanoid, its skin blacker than coal. Its face was angular, composed largely of that wide, fang-filled maw and a pair of hellish, black eyes in which tiny flames burnt and danced. Two short, bent horns sprouted from its head. In one hand it gripped a devilish weapon that looked like a set of huge, viciously-sharp garden shears fashioned from a strange, rune-adorned metal. With a dreadful singleness of purpose, it lifted this instrument of death, took it in both hands and brought both of the blades together, snapping it shut. It opened again, grinned maliciously and cut through the air once more. Threateningly, it then drew a finger across its throat and pointed at those in the circle, signalling its fiendish intent — to decapitate them all.

'Can you do anything?' Dryer begged Smith. 'We can't wait in the circle forever.'

'Yes, but first — ' Smith raised his amulet and muttered something in an arcane tongue. His next words seemed to come not from his mouth but from somewhere else: 'I've now rendered the circle silent so that the efreeti can no longer hear us. There's no point in us devising a plan if it can listen in, now is

40

there?' He helped Harris to his feet.

Dryer hesitated, unsure of how to respond.

'Feel free to speak now, Inspector.' Smith's lips seemed to be moving but Dryer was convinced that no sound was coming from them.

As though in response to this new subterfuge on the part of those within the protective circle, the efreeti vanished, became invisible.

'Fear not. My djinn can see it even if it thinks otherwise. It will alert me to its movements. However, our situation remains very precarious. The efreeti has several options whereas we have very few. The circle will not hold indefinitely so it is only too well aware that we are under siege. The Seal of Solomon will keep me safe, however, please be assured I will not abandon you and Doctor Harris. I am truly sorry that you find yourself in this situation, Inspector. A case of very unfortunate timing on your part, I'm afraid to say. You see you arrived at just the moment when I performed the incantation of summoning.'

'You . . . you mean to say you

summoned that *thing*?'

'Yes. Both Doctor Harris and myself came to the decision that we were no longer prepared to be the prey, forever hunted by the efreeti. We resolved to drawing it out where, it was hoped, we could confront it on our own terms. I must say, I was not expecting it to assume Weidenreich's guise.'

'Who is . . . was Weidenreich?' Dryer stared confusedly from Smith to Harris.

'He was an archaeologist like myself. However, he later fell in with the wrong people and became a leading occultist, a disciple of the Dark Arts. He must've sold his very soul to Pazuzu in order to become a conduit for the efreeti. Speaking of which — ' Smith turned his gaze to one side as the vengeful, evil spirit reappeared on the edge of the circle. With a savage cry it smote its weapon off some kind of invisible, unyielding, mystical barrier.

Sparks flew as it hacked down again and again.

For a moment, Dryer once more found himself mentally wrestling with the reality of all of this. It was absolutely insane, his pragmatic, rational mind shrieked at him. It had to be. He closed his eyes, willing the ghastly vision to fade away, but when he opened them, it was still there.

The efreeti, obviously reaching the conclusion that savagery and brute force would not bring down the barrier had now resorted to making foul gestures that were directed at them. It seemed to be relishing in the fact that it had them trapped.

'Why doesn't it just set the room on fire? Burn everything around us?' asked Dryer.

'It can't. As yet, it lacks a true physicality. It's unable to interact directly with the real world unless via another form of magical power. The Pazuzu heads, this protective circle or my door guardian for example. According to the research I've done over the years, this is why it is specifically after the heads. I believe that once it has 'reclaimed' all of them, by immolating those who own them it will be able to assume a true physical presence. This would spell utter disaster. It would enable the Daemon

God to re-awaken from the imprisonment the ancient Babylonian priests forced upon Him. Chaos and destruction would spread over the world on an unprecedented level. And yet . . . maybe that is the only way of ultimately defeating it.'

'What do you mean?' asked Harris. 'We can't allow it to — '

'My old friend, it may be our only means of imprisoning it once more.'

'So what can we do?' asked Harris, concernedly. There was fear stamped across his face. 'We're cursed with these damned heads. No matter how many times I've tried, I just can't get rid of it. If only that Arab fool hadn't stolen them in the first place.'

'We were all guilty of greed, back then. One can't just lay the blame on him. We all took our share of the heads, knowing full well they were archaeological relics. Admittedly we only took one each unlike some of the others. It was Weidenreich who ultimately deceived us all.'

'I don't give a damn about that,' shouted Dryer. 'Just how the hell are we going to escape? Can't your djinn or

44

whatever it is do something?' He cast a curious eye at the tall, silent figure. It had stood, motionless, like a statue, throughout their time in the circle. It was clear to him that there was a considerable amount of turbulent history between all three of them; Smith, Harris and the German. Dark deeds had been done and darker promises and oaths broken, of that he had little doubt, but ruminating over the past was not going to get them out of this problem.

'I've had another idea,' said Smith, stroking his goatee. He gave Harris a firm but friendly pat on the shoulder. 'What I do now I do in the hope that it will save both you and the Inspector.' Before the other could make offer any resistance, he shouted something to the djinn. Instantly, the tall entity vanished.

'What are you doing?' cried Harris.

Grasping his talisman, Smith, ignoring the protestations of the others, stepped outside the circle.

Dryer stared in shock and disbelief as the efreeti moved to intercept Smith. It seemed to grow in stature, becoming a flame-wreathed shadow that reared over the man, its vicious weapon raised in readiness to strike, to bring those lethal blades snapping shut.

And then, with a sharp tug, Smith broke the chain that held the Seal of Solomon and dashed it to the floor.

What happened next was to remain with Dryer for the rest of his life. For in that instant, the efreeti did bring the twin blades together, scissoring them shut with a terrible finality. Accompanied by a thick jet of blood, and a horrified scream from Harris, Smith's head was lopped off and went spiralling into the air. It landed with a sickening thud on the floor. And then, the dark shadow seemed to engulf its victim, transforming the headless body, which was still stood upright, into a blazing pillar of fire, a human candle.

Like some bizarre flaming sacrificial effigy, Smith's body remained standing as the flames turned from red to deep orange to green and then blue. This was a mystical fire, heatless and, even as Dryer stared fixedly, he was startled to see that Smith's arms were still moving, weaving strange patterns in the air.

A dense, deep blue cloud seemed to gather around. The cloud became a fog. There came an unearthly scream and the room was suddenly filled with an appalling stench like that of a corrupt, cremated soul.

Through the cloud, Dryer saw the headless body crumble. One moment it was there, the next it just seemed to disintegrate. The cloud dissipated. And in that instant, there was an almost tangible reduction in air pressure and he knew that the power of the magic circle had also gone. All that remained of Smith was now a heap of slightly glowing embers. Resting atop them was one of the fused, molten, bronze heads.

There was no sign of the efreeti.

'What? What happened?' asked Dryer, eyes staring wildly from his head. Everything seemed so terribly fantastic, nightmarish. There was a whirling, raging chaos within his brain that threatened to pull him apart. He grasped his head in his hands and with wooden steps staggered from the circle.

'Be not alarmed.'

Dryer and Harris turned. The voice had come from Smith's severed head, which now lay in the centre of a pool of dark blood, which had stained the thick carpet. There was a bright blue intensity in the eyes.

'The efreeti is bound once more. By permitting the djinn to possess me I have been able to contain it, force it back to the realm from which such beings come. Alas, I can feel my power waning. Farewell Doctor Harris, my friend . . . and goodbye to you too, Inspector.' The bright sparkle in the eyes dwindled and then went out as though extinguished.

'I . . . I don't — ' Dryer stumbled to one side, managed to support himself on a cabinet.

Harris reached into his pocket and removed the one remaining Pazuzu head. He hesitated for a moment, examining it once more as though noting something strange about it. It was as he was doing so that it began to melt, the bronze flowing like super-heated wax despite the fact that it emitted no heat. The liquid bronze became rivulets that ran between his fingers before dripping to the carpet and disappearing, signalling that the thirty-year curse was finally over.

2

SOULS OF THE FROZEN

*There was something encased in
the glacier that even the gods had
reason to fear.*

A cold, heavy rain had been falling constantly over the Norwegian port of Bergen for the past five days. It was late October and the memories of the brief, pleasant summer were long gone, the townsfolk having now resigned themselves to the long, dark winter months to come. The beautiful, rugged Scandinavian coast was subjected to torrential downpours, and it was a well accepted and indeed demonstrable phenomenon that the harsh climate moulded the Norwegian psyche — as much in the modern era as it had done in the age of the Vikings. It tended to make the people strong and resourceful but, in some, this also made them dour and unfriendly, irascible and untrusting.

Professor Kurt Eriksson, renowned glaciologist, was one such individual. Tall and broad-shouldered, with a huge white bushy beard and a shock of grey hair, he looked like a man who could have stepped from the ancient sagas. His temperament was unsurprisingly volatile and, even at sixty-two, he had more energy and physical presence than most men half his age, thinking nothing of his five-mile daily hikes. He had lost the sight in his right eye after having been struck by shrapnel from a German grenade in 1940 when he had fought in the Norwegian resistance, and consequently, he wore an eye-patch. It was this old war wound and his overall appearance that had earned him the name 'Odin' after the All-Father of the Norse pantheon.

His constantly grim demeanour matched his thoughts this time as Eriksson was privately worried. It had now been three days since he had heard anything from his expedition team — all experienced climatologists — who were based at the small research facility some one hundred

51

miles north-east, high up in the Scandinavian mountains. Safety protocol required any team working in that remote area to radio in daily, however briefly. It was here, on the remote Jotunheimen ice field, that his team of experts were conducting a range of scientific tests; gathering data and information that he would later analyse and process back at the University in Oslo. There had been certain strange anomalies in the dynamics of the glacial formations that he believed warranted further investigation and having considered several of the aerial photographs which had been taken earlier in the year he was convinced there was something unusual going on.

Shrugging off the wet and the cold, Eriksson strolled into the grounds of the Bergen environmental unit annexed to the University. With barely a nod to the passing scientists and students, he stomped straight up to a glass-fronted door and pushed it open.

A tall, fair-haired, bespectacled man looked up in surprise from the desk at which he sat.

'Don't bother with any pleasantries, Larsen,' said the professor brusquely. 'I'm not in the mood.' He slumped down into a chair opposite and fixed the other with a dark glower. 'What do you think should be done next?'

'I'm not sure.' Doctor Harald Larsen shrugged his thin shoulders. He was well aware of the situation; after all he was third in charge of the department after Doctor Albert Landsberg, who was out on the field, and of course Eriksson.

'Great! I thought as much on the train coming over from Oslo.' Eriksson removed a silver-plated hipflask from an inner coat pocket, unscrewed the cap and took a hearty drink. The neat liquor burnt his gullet as it went down, filling his stomach with a pleasurable and very welcome glow.

'Surely the logical thing to do now would be to inform the police? The fact that we've been unable to receive any form of contact from the base headquarters could mean that something disastrous has happened.'

'Come now. Let's not leap to such drastic conclusions. Not yet at any rate.

You're too much of a catastrophist, Larsen. We all know what the weather can be like up there. It would only take one severe snowstorm to render much of the wireless equipment unusable. And if there has been a heavy snowfall then the track down from the base would become quite unusable.'

'Well, you're in charge. What do you suggest?'

Eriksson took another drink from his hipflask before returning it to his pocket. For a moment he sat quite still, gently chewing his bottom lip. It was clear that he had no real idea what to do next.

'Well?' prompted Larsen.

'I'm thinking.' The professor ran a hand through his dense beard. He straightened. 'How soon could we get another team ready?'

'*Another team?*' Larsen looked momentarily confused. 'I don't know. Most of the experts are out there at the moment.' He thought things over quickly, cogitating how many skilled and trained personnel remained at the unit. 'There aren't that many left at our disposal.' *Disposal*. Now there was a word he didn't like the sound of. It had too many negative connotations and considering the current situation . . . He swallowed involuntarily. 'I'd say we could put together sufficient numbers in four, maybe five days.'

'Not good enough,' Eriksson growled. 'We can't afford to wait that long. If they are stuck up there it's imperative that we get to them fast.'

'If they're still alive.'

Eriksson fixed Larsen with a hard stare.

'I think it's sheer madness not to get the police involved. As a bare minimum, at least get the local rescue teams mobilised. I'm sure there must be a mountain rescue centre based at Skjolden or somewhere else in the vicinity.'

Eriksson gave out a deep sigh. He lumbered to his feet like a grizzly bear. 'We will, I assure you. But not quite yet. After all, it's only been three days. The last thing I want is to attract unwanted publicity at this stage. As you will no doubt recall, it took a hell of a lot of persuasion on my part to obtain the necessary funding from the university. So the last thing — '

'Good God, man! People's lives may be at risk and you're more concerned with how the university will react. It's insane. Get your priorities in order.' There were flashes of uncommon anger in Larsen's eyes.

'Don't think for one minute that I'm jeopardising personnel safety for the sake of my own reputation. I just think we can do this ourselves. If the radios are simply out we would be wasting the emergency services' time. I want to assess the situation first-hand.' Eriksson shambled over to a large map on the wall. He studied it briefly. 'Depending on the traffic, and of course the weather, we could get to Skjolden in about five hours.'

Larsen uttered a humourless laugh. 'And then what?'

The professor turned, focusing his one-eyed vision on his colleague. 'We can make plans once we get there. I'm certain that we can get to the bottom of this without having to involve any of the authorities.'

'I can't say that I approve.' Larsen removed his glasses and cleaned them with a handkerchief before putting them back on. 'It sounds absolute folly to me.'

'You're just going to have to trust me on this.' Eriksson turned his gaze back to the map. He stared at the mountainous area depicted, calling on his knowledge and imagination, mentally picturing the snow-covered landscape that could be filled with frozen death and desolation, trying hard to dismiss the dark thoughts that crawled insidiously through his mind when it came to the fate of his expedition team.

Jotunheimen. The Land of the Giants. A glacial, rugged world, set apart, isolated from the mortal realm by its sheer bleakness and altitude.

★ ★ ★

Once the hurried preparations were put in place, Eriksson and Larsen left the relative sanity of Bergen and drove out from the bustling residential areas into the harsh grimness of the Norwegian countryside, the going becoming increasingly treacherous. They were soon heading high into the

57

surrounding foothills, the Norwegian Sea a dark and capricious sprawl behind them.

The vehicle in which they travelled was a huge, modern, state-of-the-art, all-terrain jeep that had been specially modified for coping with the difficult driving conditions. It was a true monster of a machine that belonged to the Environmental Survey Department and it made light work of the numerous twisting hairpin bends and sharp uphill roads.

Larsen cast a glance into the rear of the vehicle. They had stashed an ample supply of tinned foodstuffs and camping gear. In addition, there was a wealth of environmental and geological surveying equipment and gadgetry.

'Well, we've got more than enough to ensure the running of the camp, presuming that there's still a camp there by the time we arrive.'

'I've told you to stop being a doom-monger.' Eriksson shifted gear in order to begin a sudden climb. 'Of course the camp will still be there. You'll see. There's just been a breakdown in communication, that's all. Talking of which, why don't you keep the airwaves open on the radio to the emergency frequency just in case we get any feedback. We'll stop every half hour or so in order for you to try to regain contact on the off-chance that we'll get a better signal the nearer we get to them.'

They drove higher and higher into the surrouding mountains; the landscape altering drastically as it continued to become more spectacular. A slight improvement in the weather enabled better visibility but they both knew it wouldn't last long. Eriksson had made this journey many times and it never ceased to amaze and impress him. It was almost like going through time; the low foothills, nearer the coast, with their green valleys and scattered villages were still autumnal, whereas in the higher mountains it was distinctly wintry — frozen, barren and unforgiving. Yet he knew these roads like the back of his own hand. He was well acquainted with their dangers and their hidden treachery.

This was a land immersed in myth and legend and surveying the world about him it was easy for Eriksson to understand how it had given rise to the fierce and often brutal worship of the Old Norse gods. This was without doubt a world that many in the past — and some equally superstitious people in the present — believed to be inhabited by trolls and dragons, malign shape-changers and angry, elemental spirits. He had heard some of the subtle and horrible things spoken of only in whispers in the villages of the lowlands. Of the black, formless, dead things that rode on the icy wind and hurled their shrieking vengeance from the tall mountaintops.

Rounding a high bend they were presented with an awe-inspiring panorama as far below them stretched a great, deep-blue fjord, its steep-sided cliff walls broken here and there by spectacular waterfalls. Low-level grey rain clouds began to mass and abruptly a light fog enveloped the vehicle.

Eriksson switched on the powerful headlights and continued to drive. Providing the weather did not deteriorate further and the roads remained clear of avalanches — a frequent hazard in these higher altitudes — he hoped to reach Skjolden before sunset.

'I don't know if I should be saying this, but what are your thoughts on Landsberg?'

Larsen's question took the professor completely by surprise. He cocked his head slightly, maintaining a tight grip on the steering wheel. 'What do you mean?'

The other hesitated for a moment, obviously unsure how to frame his response. 'Well, it's just that I've never been too keen on him.'

'He's a competent enough scientist,' said Eriksson.

'Yes, I know. One of the best. However it's his personality and his, *beliefs*, that I'm not so sure about.'

'His beliefs?'

'Surely you know that he's a pagan.'

'Can't say that I did.' Eriksson wasn't particularly interested. He himself was a staunch atheist; believing only in the laws of nature and physics. He was first and foremost a rationalist, a war-hardened pragmatist who had no time for idle fantasies or unsubstantiated religious ideology. 'Anyway, as far as I'm concerned, he can worship little green men from Mars so long as his scientific work remains as good as it has been. He's one of the top glaciologists in Europe. That paper he wrote about the accumulation versus ablation ratios of the Briksdalsbreen Glacier was one of the best I've ever read.'

'Hmm. Still, I just find it a trifle odd that a man can still adhere to those old beliefs in this day and age,' mused Larsen. 'That's something that just doesn't sit comfortably with me.'

'Each to their own, I say.' Eriksson turned on the powerful windscreen wipers to deal with the light snow that began to fall. 'I didn't think that the snow would hit us this early but you never can tell. The local forecast mentioned the possibility but we know how wrong they can be.' He switched on to a local radio station in the hope of getting a weather update. After about ten minutes of meaningless reporting, the broadcaster informed them that the afternoon was scheduled to remain rainy with only sporadic snow showers on the higher ground. However, even as the report was coming to an end, the snow began to thicken, becoming almost blizzard-like; great white, icy flurries obscuring vision and eddying into blinding whirlwinds all around them.

What other traffic they saw was now crawling, covered in snow. Everyone had their headlights on full beam and Eriksson and his passenger noted with growing concern and alarm the rapid darkening of the skies. Rain, interspersed with hailstones and snow, battered their vehicle as they ploughed ever higher, each difficult mile bringing them closer to their destination.

Some three hours after leaving Bergen, they came to a narrow stretch of road that had been half-buried by a minor landfall at which road crews were working efficiently and flat-out, trying to clear the obstruction. It took the best part of an hour and a half for the road to reopen during which time the two men had sat in the back of their vehicle and drunk coffee, stopping occasionally to fiddle with the radio controls in order to try and make contact with the base headquarters. They had no success.

When the way was clear they set off again.

Each of them carried their own fears and apprehensions about just what they were going to encounter when they eventually reached the base camp.

Eriksson steadfastly clung to the belief that there was nothing seriously amiss. That there had been but a communication problem — something that he himself had experienced on several occasions whilst working at such remote and largely inaccessible locations. Unlike Larsen, he wouldn't dwell on the darker possibilities, holding to the view that all of those in question were competent scientific men who not only knew these mountains almost as well as he did but were also highly capable, equipped to deal with any misfortune that may have arisen. And yet, despite his relative optimism, there remained that germ of nagging apprehension within the pit of his stomach — that small, unshakeable trace of worry that even now began to fester and grow with each passing hour.

The remainder of the journey to Skjolden passed in an almost deathly silence as both driver and passenger ruminated on their fears. Outside, the darkness of mid-afternoon began to encroach down from the mountains instilling within them a deepening sense of despair and depression almost as though the sombre state inside the vehicle had been given substance and had become mirrored in the gloom of the shadow-filled landscape that loomed menacingly and forebodingly all around them.

It was with some relief that the village of Skjolden seemed to materialise out of the virtual whiteout.

★   ★   ★

Eriksson ordered himself and Larsen two medium-rare whale steaks and returned from the bar carrying a large stein of lager. He walked over to where his colleague sat and sank down into the chair opposite.

'Well we're here. Now what?' Larsen asked, sharply.

The professor took a sip of his drink, nodded approvingly and took a hearty swallow. He put it down and looked at the other, clearly annoyed and frustrated. 'I wish to God that you'd relax a little bit more.'

'Maybe when we've discovered what's happened to our expedition members.'

'You know what your problem is, don't you?' Eriksson spoke bluntly, not really intending to cause offence but not that bothered either way. 'You've got too much of an overactive imagination. You're bound to imagine the worst. No doubt in your mind they've all fallen down some deep crevasse, or maybe they've been beset by wolves, perhaps even trolls. Hell, no doubt you think they may have unearthed some alien horror that's been encased in the ice for thousands of years.'

'And you think *I've* got an overactive imagination?' Larsen looked at the other with an unfriendly stare. He was about to comment further when he saw a waitress coming over with their food.

Their dinner was a meal of uncomfortable silences. It was an awkward experience for both of them and to a casual observer it was abundantly clear that neither enjoyed the other's company. This was clearly a meeting forged by necessity rather than friendship.

Once their meal was over it was time to get down to business. They were now within twenty miles of the base headquarters in terms of physical distance but they both knew that their team members may as well have been on a different planet, such was the remote glacial alienness which separated the two.

'At first light I'll make some enquiries to see if there are any local guides who would be willing to accompany us up the mountain,' said Eriksson. 'I would have thought that there would be someone who would want to earn a few extra kronar.'

'I wouldn't hold out much hope,' replied Larsen pessimistically. 'Skjolden is a small village. Most of its inhabitants are elderly and as you are no doubt only too well aware they're not that keen on outsiders.' He glanced meaningfully towards the innkeeper and the half-dozen elderly patrons gathered around the bar who eyed them suspiciously. 'This place has 'strangers not welcome' written all over it. I bet they hardly get any outside custom at all.'

The professor waited for the waitress to clear the empty plates away before continuing the conversation. 'Well, that being the case, we'll just have to go up the mountain on our own. We know the way. We'll go as far as we can in the jeep and then head off on foot if need be.' He clambered to his feet. 'Well, I plan on having a few more drinks before turning in for the night. It's been a long day.'

* * *

Not surprisingly, they could interest no one in accompanying them. Eriksson couldn't help but feel that those few whom he had raised the issue with were frightened; scared almost. It wasn't so much the harsh climate or the prospect of tackling the road that seemed to be behind such irrational fear but rather something altogether more indefinable.

The villagers spoke of terrible things having been done up there, both recently and in the dim and distant past. It was a bad place with a wicked reputation, they said. Many unsuspecting folk, mostly climbers and tourists, had disappeared having gone up there. Folklore told of monsters born of nightmare who wandered the snow-covered wilderness; mighty frost giants that murdered and devoured their victims raw.

'If you go up there you're only asking for bad trouble and ill luck,' muttered one old-timer who sat out on his porch. The old man was lined and grizzled and wore a bizarre wolverine fur hat. He stank of uncooked herring and cheap ale. 'There be monsters that even the Old Gods couldn't bring themselves to face. So they buried them in the ice hoping to contain them until the end of time. To keep them there until the days of Ragnarok. People nowadays, folk like yourselves, think you know everything with your science and your new gadgets and that may be fine enough for the towns and the cities but it all counts for nothing when you're up there at night and you can hear the mad howls that come down from the mountains. You go ask the folk at Yorvaskr. I dare you. They'll tell you what I'm on about.'

'Yorvaskr?' Eriksson was unfamiliar with the name.

'The little village just on the near side of Mount Galdhøpiggen. You won't find it on any map so there's no point you looking. I've only been there once and it was nigh on fifty years ago. Some say it no longer exists and that it's uninhabited, but I'm not so sure. Little more than a cluster of houses. It's cut off for most of the year. In fact the trail to it only opens two or three weeks during the summer or so I've heard. Still, that beast of a machine you drove into Skjolden with yesterday might get you there.'

'I'm afraid I've got no time for superstitious nonsense,' replied Eriksson. 'We're scientists, not fools. We're members of an expeditionary team. Our fellow members are based up there and we haven't heard from them for several days. We've come to check on them and to ensure their well-being.'

'Well, as I guessed, it looks like it's just going to be us.' There was a certain degree of mockery in Larsen's voice. 'Come on. The sooner we get out of this place the better. Hell, right now I think I'd much rather be up on the ice-field. Anywhere, but here.'

Eriksson grumbled a curse. With a dismissive shake of his shaggy head, he turned and, shoulders hunched, headed off in the direction of their parked vehicle.

A minute later they were driving out of Skjolden, the snow-chained tyres crunching through the densely-packed snow. And then they were turning off the main route, taking a much lesser track that meandered into the white wilderness.

The sky was brightening as a late morning sun battled to shine through the grey clouds. After twenty minutes or so, the going became increasingly difficult and, rounding a vast upthrusting rocky spur, the world around them altered dramatically. Before them, as far as the eye could see, stretched a glacial, almost otherworldly, vista of towering, snow-capped peaks. The higher mountains were half-hidden by wisps of constantly shifting cloud that added to the overall strangeness and alien enchantment.

'We're getting near now,' commented Larsen. Like the professor, he had been here several times before but the scenery never ceased to amaze him and instil within him a strong sense of wonder.

'Yes. It can't be far now to the base. Another couple of miles at most, if memory serves me right. I must say I'm a little concerned that there are no tracks or anything visible. I'd have thought Landsberg or one of his team would have been able to get down if needed.'

The snow was becoming deeper but providing they steered clear of any large drifts, Eriksson hoped to get the jeep all the way to the camp. And yet, despite his sense of optimism, the very fact that so far there were no other signs of life sparked the sense of unease within his brain. There was something wrong here, cried out that disquieting inner voice. With a fearful, dry swallow he tightened his grip on the steering wheel and kept going.

★ ★ ★

Eriksson looked hard at his companion, the concern and incredulity on his own face mirrored, almost down to the smallest detail, that on the other's. With a puzzled, disbelieving shrug of his broad shoulders, he shambled from one deserted porta-cabin to another, now absolutely convinced that something unfathomable and down-right bizarre had occurred here.

For there was no sign of anyone. No frozen corpses. No hastily scribbled messages. No tracks, be they footprints or tyre or ski marks or imprints. The general impression, certainly after a cursory search of the facility buildings, was that although the camp had not been left in a hurry, it had not been occupied for the last few days.

Clad in their fur-lined parka coats, the two men staggered from empty building to empty building as overhead the skies darkened ominously.

There was something almost surreal about all of this that Eriksson could not comprehend. This was unlike anything he had ever experienced before — something his pragmatism and his scientific mind and rationale were incapable of analysing and coming to terms with. It just didn't make any sense and no matter how hard he tried, he just couldn't theorise any plausible explanation that would provide an answer.

In the main office they uncovered Landsberg's logbook and although it proved that the team had been here as scheduled, the entries ceased three days ago.

'Do you think they just left?' ventured Larsen.

Eriksson didn't know what to think. How on earth could the entire team just leave without any notice? And yet he privately hoped that this was the answer, for the other possible alternatives did not sit comfortably with him. If they hadn't left, then in all likelihood they had all perished up on the glacier or somewhere out there in the frozen wastes.

'There's the radio equipment.' Larsen walked over to the large table in one corner. He flicked a switch and the wireless unit crackled into life. Checking it, he found it to be in order. 'Works fine. In fact it's quite a strong signal,' he said, turning to the professor. 'This is getting stranger and stranger. All it needed was to be switched on.'

Eriksson sank into a chair. He rested his head in his hands, mentally wrestling over how to proceed. He looked up at his companion. 'Let's try and look at this objectively. We know that Landsberg and his team were here. We know that the radio equipment's working and we know that whatever happened, it happened some three days ago.' He scratched worriedly at his head. 'Do you think they could've gone to this godforsaken hamlet that superstitious fool mentioned?'

'What on earth for?' None of this made any sense to Larsen. He would have found it far easier to accept things had they found the entire team dead from hypothermia for he had all but prepared himself for such. But this — this was utterly inexplicable.

Eriksson pushed himself to his feet, a look of determination on his face. 'Alright. Now's the time to get the authorities involved. You get whatever emergency service you can on the radio. Tell them everything. Explain to them that we're up here and that there's no sign of the Oslo-Bergen glacial research expedition based at Jotunheimen. Tell them to get a rescue team out here as soon as possible.'

'A rescue team? There's no one here to rescue.'

'Not yet, but I think we should head up to the glacier to see if there's any sign of —

'Survivors?'

Eriksson nodded. 'Well, get on with it. I'm going to take a final look around.' He headed for the door. Upon opening it, he was struck by an icy blast of freezing air. Snow flurried inside. He raised his hood and went out slamming the door behind him.

Everything was too still, too quiet. The

silence unnerved him. Reaching into his inner coat pocket, he withdrew his hip-flask, unscrewed the lid and took a drink. He knew fine well that alcohol and sub-zero temperatures weren't the best of mixtures but right now he was past caring.

It was perhaps the loneliness and the absolute sense of isolation that, more than anything else, was causing the sense of anxiety. There was no one here but himself and Larsen. No one at all. Or so it seemed. Fear gripped his heart and mind with icy, sadistic talons. Trying to shake off the mood, he strode off towards the nearest out-building.

A sudden dark movement, stark against the overall whiteness, made him stop in mid-stride. He turned swiftly, heart thumping, certain that the dark flash he had seen in the corner of his eye had not been due to his overwrought imagination.

'Hello!' he called, hoping that it was one of his team members. He waited for several seconds but there was no response. 'Hello! Is there anyone there? It's Professor Eriksson.' With a deep sense of apprehension, he walked over to where several fuel drums had been placed.

There was nothing. There weren't even footprints in the snow!

He stared perplexedly at the ground before backing away. Some distance behind him a door slammed shut.

'Eriksson! Eriksson!'

There was no mistaking the desperation and horror in Larsen's scream.

Eriksson turned and rushed back to see Larsen stumbling towards him out of the growing blizzard. The look on his face was unlike any he had ever seen on a human being before. All of the colour had drained from it and the eyes were wide, almost bulging from his head.

'There was a — ' Larsen seemed incapable of getting any more information out.

'A what?' Eriksson trudged forward and gripped the other by the shoulders. 'Damn it, man. What is it? What happened?'

Larsen was petrified. His mouth moved but nothing coherent came from his lips. He raised a visibly trembling hand to his face.

'Snap out of it!' Eriksson shook him fiercely and then he staggered back as he saw a dark figure emerge from the door Larsen had just fled from.

The thing was man-like, dressed similarly to them in a heavy parka coat — *but the face!* Its features were a sickly combination of everything hellish and unwholesome; decayed and unliving, twin pinpoints of evil-red, glaring eyes fixing them with a malevolent intent. Frozen flesh, brittle and glassy and a fang-filled mouth that screamed at them. Wisps of icy-bluish steam rose from its body as the terrible sound rent the deathly silence.

Both men withdrew as the ghastly abomination advanced towards them, purple-veined hands clenched in livid anger. It had the semblance of a corpse that had just stepped from a freezer.

It was now less than twenty yards away and Eriksson could see that, despite its grotesqueness, it was — or perhaps had been — one of his expedition personnel. He could not remember the name of the individual but he was certain that this was not some demon born of nightmare but rather a tainted, perhaps diseased, human being. With a sense of revulsion, he saw the drool leak and slather from the now open and unfrozen mouth. With horror, he reasoned that it was salivating at the prospect of eating them.

'Just keep backing away,' Eriksson said, trying to keep his voice steady. 'If he charges us we make a dash for the jeep.' When Larsen made no reply, the professor grabbed him by the sleeve and hauled him back.

Suddenly, with a gargling scream, Larsen shook free of the professor's grasp and made off, floundering through the shin-deep snow.

As though that had been the signal, the advancing, frozen-faced ghoul began bounding towards them, its arms outstretched.

Fear lent Eriksson strength. With a cry, he turned and began his ungainly flight through the snow. Up ahead, he could see Larsen stumbling and screaming like a madman in his bid to escape. Still some distance ahead was the jeep. If they could only —

A second, parka-coated nightmare appeared from behind the vehicle!

A third and then a fourth began to drag themselves from beneath the snow, before clambering to their feet, blocking the escape route, their hideous, corrupted faces filled with utter malignity.

Panic thrust its way into Eriksson, spearing into his heart. He stumbled to his knees in despair. Larsen staggered back towards him, still mumbling insane words. It was fairly clear that he was now on the verge of full-blown insanity.

Now that they had their prey encircled, the zombie-like creatures approached more stealthily, closing in from every direction.

Suddenly a shot rang out.

Eriksson turned. From one of the supply sheds that they hadn't explored stepped a man. He was dressed in much the same way as the others and the professor immediately recognised Doctor Albert Landsberg. In one hand Landsberg carried a revolver.

'*Landsberg!* Save us! Shoot these hell-fiends.'

Landsberg fixed Eriksson with an odd stare. He began to come towards him. There was neither fear nor alarm in his eyes despite the proximity of the dreadful, gibbering, diseased ones gathered around. It was almost as though he viewed them still as fellow scientists.

'What's going on here?' asked Eriksson. 'What happened?'

'*What happened*? Why only the greatest discovery ever.' Landsberg walked closer. 'I've known for years that there's power here buried in the glacier. Untold, ancient power.' There were unconstrained glints of madness in his eyes. 'If you only knew.'

'Power? Glacial power? What are you on about?'

Landsberg laughed. '*Glacial power*? Hah! The power I speak of is not restricted to carving valleys and eroding mountains. I speak of an entity that can and will destroy the world.'

'You're mad. Just like these mindless things around us. What happened here? We should leave and get help. Perhaps with skilled treatment — '

'You think *they* can be cured? Impossible. Besides, what makes you think they, and the others, would want to be cured? They have now offered their very souls to that which lies encased nearby.'

'What? What are you talking about? For the love of God, Landsberg — '

'*The love of God?* I have the love of my god as do those around you. The offspring of Loki were scattered and buried, left to die or await that appointed time when the faithful would awaken them. Such a time draws near. The villagers of Yorvaskr have sought to keep this holy site safe for generations. It was they who informed me of what had to be done. Consider yourself fortunate, for before this night is out I shall introduce you to them.'

This was absolute lunacy, thought Eriksson. Sheer, concentrated madness. Landsberg was clearly insane, beyond reason and as such his and Larsen's only hope of survival was to flee, but as things stood that was nigh on impossible. The moment they made a dash for it either Landsberg's fanatical zombies would be upon them or they would be shot — the latter of the two would be by far the more merciful. Eriksson's dilemma was compounded by the fact that Larsen was not fully in possession of his faculties.

'What do you intend to do? Kill us?'

Landsberg smiled cruelly. 'Maybe. So, if you'll both kindly come with me.' He gestured with his gun.

The hideous man-things growled and eyed Eriksson hungrily.

Suddenly Landsberg shouted something in a language Eriksson had never heard before and instantly his four minions rushed forward, grabbing the professor and the hapless Larsen, their very touch chilling the two men to the bone.

Up close, Eriksson was revolted at the foul stench his captors exuded. Savagely, he fought back the urge to vomit as he was roughly manhandled and frog-marched into one of the smaller supply buildings, basically no more than a windowless shed.

Once inside, Landsberg dismissed his grotesque accomplices and closed the door behind him. With his revolver trained on the professor, he gestured for him to sit down. Larsen crouched nearby, tugging at his hair and shaking uncontrollably.

'And so it came to pass that Utgard-Loki, alone of all the frost giants, came to learn the means of reawakening the Earth-encircling serpent Jormungandr, the second born offspring of Loki and Angrboda.' Landsberg talked clinically and precisely, his words delivered as though he was giving a lecture. A cold smile formed on his lips upon noting the confusion on his listener's face but he continued regardless: 'He's here, Eriksson! I've found Him in the glacier! All along, the ignorant have consigned the ancient beliefs to the realm of myth and legend. Fables told by ancient people to instil courage into the hearts of their warriors and frighten children at bedtime. Science has tried to extinguish the fires of belief, enabling men like you and that snivelling wretch at your side to go through life oblivious to the reality that there *are* beings far more powerful than we. To think that some called you 'Odin' whilst all along you've ridiculed the very concept of worship of the Old Gods. Know that before you die you will be forced to accept their existence. Soon I will have the power to revive Utgard-Loki and with His aid Jormungandr will rise and devour the world!'

An avalanche of thoughts and emotions crashed and tumbled within Eriksson's mind. He had sat and listened to his former colleague rant and rave with such fervour that for a few moments he didn't know what was truth and what was fiction. He was dumbstruck, unable to comprehend the situation. This was madness. It had to be. A thought suddenly sprang into his mind — perhaps it was all a long, protracted nightmare from which he would awaken, gripping the pillow and lathered in a cold sweat. He was only dimly aware that the other was speaking again.

'The men who came here have been altered by my sorcery. Through my worship of the goddess Hel, the daughter of Loki, I was able to . . . transform them. They are what you could consider *zombies*. Their souls have been frozen and offered to Utgard-Loki. Raising the dead is not just the preserve of Haitian voodoo-priests. Indeed, my sorcery is older, far older.'

'You're insane. Completely and utterly.' Eriksson had at last found his voice.

'*Insane?*' Landsberg mused. 'Yes. Perhaps I am.' He laughed mirthlessly. 'Tell you what, 'Odin'. I'll show you just how *insane* I am.' In a quick movement, he raised his revolver and shot three bullets into Larsen.

'*No!*' Eriksson yelled, his face spattered with his companion's blood. He looked down at the dead and bleeding body at his feet. A sudden surge of anger sprang him upright as he prepared to launch himself at the cold-blooded murderer; to clasp his hands around his throat and squeeze the life from him.

Landsberg pulled back several steps, shaking his head. 'I know what you're thinking but remember, I've got two bullets left.' He pointed the gun at the professor's head. '*Sit down!*'

Eriksson was shaking all over with adrenaline, fear and rage. His hands knotted into fists of iron. 'You murder-ing — ' He struggled to finish but it was abundantly clear what he wanted to say. Resignedly, he slumped back into his chair.

'He was disposable. Useless. Even as a scientist he was completely incompetent. Why, if I remember rightly you yourself ridiculed much of his work.' Landsberg gazed indifferently at the man he had just killed before looking directly at the professor. 'You on the other hand are needed for the final sacrifice. When night falls, you're coming up to the glacier. And then, well believe me, I think you'd rather your and Larsen's fates were reversed.'

'You'll pay for this Landsberg,' spat Eriksson. 'You'll spend the rest of your life in jail.'

'You still don't get it, do you? You think that the prospect of a jail sentence bothers me? Don't you realise what I'm going to do? I'm going to bring about the end of the world.'

Eriksson gulped. There was so much conviction in the madman's eyes that it seemed just possible that he *was* telling the truth. Either that or the strength with which Landsberg believed his own delusion was so powerful that it was rubbing off on those around him. However he tried to analyse it, it was certainly a troubling thought.

'I'll return for you later.' Landsberg left the building and locked the door.

★ ★ ★

During his time of isolation and captivity, numerous contrasting emotions and thoughts raced through Eriksson's mind. For a time, he tried to convince himself, unsuccessfully, that none of this was actually happening. It was so unreal. And yet, the images of Larsen, dead and bullet-ridden and the horrible faces of his expedition team members wouldn't leave him, no matter how hard he tried to erase them from his consciousness.

Despite the fact that the building he was in was a supply shed, he found little that was of any practical use, leading him to believe that most of the equipment had been transferred elsewhere. However, he did manage to find a small flare gun,

89

which he concealed inside his coat. In a drawer he also found a large chisel, which at a push could be used as a weapon. This he also secreted in his coat.

At one stage, his hopes had lifted upon hearing what he thought was the sounds of a circling helicopter and he had wrestled with the decision whether or not to try and break down the door in order to signal his distress. After the sounds had stopped, he had silently cursed himself for not having at least attempted to break free. He didn't think he would get a second chance, not considering Larsen's diabolical intentions.

★　★　★

Some three hours later, he heard the sound of footsteps nearing the door. With a click, a key turned in the lock and Landsberg pushed the door open. Outside, it was pitch black and it had clearly been snowing heavily.

'Well, 'Odin', it's time.' Landsberg pulled his gun from his coat pocket. 'Let's go.'

Any thoughts of escape fled instantly

from Eriksson's mind when two of the frozen-faced things stepped into the doorway. Hands grabbed him, holding him in a grip as cold as death. Landsberg then shouted a strange command and the undead servants dragged the professor outside.

Eriksson struggled for a moment before realising the futility. There was no way he was going to break free. With a sense of resignation, he chose to reserve his energy in the hope that a more optimum time came for the possibility of escape.

'Come on. We walk from here.' Landsberg switched on a powerful torch and led the way out of the camp. He swung the beam from side to side, illuminating the barely discernible route that he intended to take, the densely-packed snow on either side forming high lumps that loomed in the darkness like ancient, icy burial mounds. A strong wind, laden with snow, gusted down the mountainside.

Soon they were climbing, the snow now knee-high, their progress becoming slower. Despite the fur-lined heavy coat Eriksson wore, the cold was severe, perishingly cold; a freezing chill that stung the nose, throat and lungs with each breath. He could no longer feel his toes.

Vast, upthrusting pinnacles of rock protruded from the glacial landscape like the jagged, serrated teeth of buried dragons, their rugged surfaces glistening with snow when caught in the torchlight. Half-seen, wraith-like things seemed to cavort within the blizzard, staying just on the periphery of their light source. In the shadowy darkness, the looming wall of the glacier they were now approaching lost much of its immense grandeur. Yet, even still, Eriksson could make out the towering mass of ice which stretched high into the night sky and he knew that it extended for some twenty miles across the Jotunheimen expanse; an incredibly thick and enormous ice sheet that had lain here since the time of the last Ice Age some ten thousand years ago. Was it truly all that surprising that something could remain, preserved, buried within; encased throughout the millennia in an icy prison?

Eriksson could see that this region of the glacier they were nearing had been hewn; excavated by picks and blasted in places with small explosive charges. A carved tunnel made its way into its icy interior. The work had been crude and hurried and yet he stared in awe at the scale of the undertaking for the frozen passage stretched far into the incredible mass of ice, disappearing well out of the range of the torch.

'Get moving.' Landsberg shoved the professor hard on the back causing him to stumble slightly.

They all entered. The temperature dropped considerably, to such an extent that Eriksson feared getting sudden frostbite with exposure of his skin to the faceted, tunnelled-out glacial surfaces, which reflected and refracted the torch-light as though it were polished crystal. However this was an unearthly cold, a teeth-chattering bitterness that gnawed at the heart and the soul. If it were going to get any colder, Eriksson was certain it would bring him to a complete standstill; encase him in the ice, freeze him solid

— turn him into nothing more than a lifeless sculpture.

They had been going for almost two hundred yards when the hewn-out passage which had been going almost level as far as Eriksson could tell, began to slope down. It widened, becoming almost cavernous in proportion. In spite of his predicament, his eyes widened as he tried to take in the view becoming more visible before him. It was unbelievable, he tried to tell himself; fantastical — a vast hollow chamber within the very glacier, which had clearly not been excavated by Landsberg or his helpers. Rather, this was something that had been here for a very, very long time; a primordial burial site fit for something not of this world.

Skulls and bones belonging to all manner of things lay strewn all over the ground, and a strange greenish luminescence seemed to glow from the very ice walls, illuminating the huge area in a weird, unearthly light. Dark shapes loped and shuffled amidst the bones. They were bipedal and human-like in their movement, but as Eriksson was brought closer his face contorted in disgust when he saw the things more clearly.

'I told you I would introduce you to the inhabitants of Yorvaskr,' said Landsberg.

Eriksson almost lost his sanity there, staring at the degenerate creatures. More than anything they put him in mind of ghouls — corpse-eating horrors. Only his intense rage at Landsberg was keeping the terror at bay. 'Are they human?' he managed to ask.

'More or less, I'd say. I've been visiting Yorvaskr for thirty years and only a favoured few evolve this way.' Landsberg answered.

Favoured? Eriksson shivered. There was not a trace of irony in the madman's tone.

'About one in every ten are blessed in this manner, and the people rejoice at another of Loki's chosen.'

Poor wretches, thought Eriksson. There must be some genetic flaw in the Yorvaskr populace to produce these throwbacks so regularly, and then someone like Landsberg, with his deluded ideas of mythic grandeur, comes and makes things worse.

For Eriksson could see old equipment from the university that had been used to speed up the excavation. Delusions alone however, could not account for the apparent *zombification* of the expedition team.

'Come, you can see our goal before the sacrifice.' Landsberg strode towards a large fissure in the ice and the professor had no choice but to follow. They walked along an ice tunnel for a short distance before Landsberg clamped a hand on Eriksson's shoulder, He leaned in close and spoke quietly. 'Remember all that you've read of Earth's history, all the hundreds of books with their 'facts'. Now look and you will see how wrong they all were.' He swung his torch forwards to illuminate the end of the tunnel.

In the light, Eriksson began to make out shapes, just behind the ice, massive shadows. His mind struggled to make sense of the patterns, then the forms resolved themselves as he traced the outlines of bones. 'It can't be!' he exclaimed, moving forward almost involuntarily to peer at the ice.

'You see? It's true, all of it is true!' Landsberg ran his gloved hand over the ice, almost reverently. 'Utgard-Loki lies here, His body entombed in the glacier. The people of Yorvaskr have guarded it for millennia, waiting for the time when He can be restored to life. We've sacrificed many to reach this point but you will be the last. Your death by fire will finally enable me to bring life to these bones and He can break out of the remaining ice Himself. According to the writings, the last sacrifice has to be a worthy one. A man who is both warrior and wise man. Although I despise your narrow mind, I know of your intellect and I found out about your war record — both the official version and the secret file. I had to get you here at the right time to play your part.' He laughed. 'Why, even your resemblance to Odin will please my god.'

Eriksson lost him temper. 'Don't be so bloody stupid man! That thing has got to be a mammoth or something, perhaps a frozen plesiosaur. Frost giants don't exist, neither do world-eating serpents or the

97

Norse gods, and they have never done so.' In a act of sudden rage, he smashed his fist into Landsberg's face, taking the other by complete surprise. Landsberg dropped the gun as he staggered and Eriksson picked it up and ran, firing two blind shots at Landsberg. The monstrously deformed thing who had accompanied them to the fissure, Frederiksson he thought had been his name, followed him but was slow to react.

Eriksson ran for his life through the nightmarish cavern with its imbecilic inhabitants and towards the exit. Behind him, he heard Landsberg shouting orders to his slaves. There was terror and confusion in his head. Despite his angry words to Landsberg, he knew it had been no mammoth in the ice. The sheer size of the bones precluded any land animal he knew and what he had been able to make out had looked shockingly humanoid. Whatever the explanation, Landsberg was mad, and a murderer to boot, there was no doubt about that, and he had to find a way out of this nightmare.

And then he was out.

Staggering and stumbling down through the snow, Eriksson saw a light suddenly appear up ahead — headlights! A vehicle was coming slowly in his direction and he recognised the outline of a rescue jeep. He ran towards it, waving his arms frantically. Two figures jumped out of the jeep and caught him just as his strength gave way.

'We've got you now, don't worry.'

'Get him inside quickly.'

'We have to leave immediately, you have no idea.' Eriksson gasped as they carried him to the jeep. A third man climbed out, a rifle with a telescopic sight in his hands. Not quite pointing it at the professor, he began to question Eriksson even as his colleagues checked him over for injuries.

'Are you Professor Larsen?'

'No, I'm . . . '

'Where is Professor Larsen who radioed the distress call?'

'Dead, shot by Landsberg. He's completely insane.'

'Where is this Landsberg now?'

Eriksson was trembling as the shock set in. 'In the glacier, but you can't go in there, he's mad and . . . he's not alone.'

'Look, over there!' one of the rescuers pointed. In the headlights they saw a figure emerging from the barely discernible tunnel. As it approached, the face became visible and they could see the ruined features of Frederiksson.

'Shoot it, for god's sake!' yelled Eriksson, but the mountain rescue team tried to calm him as one of them went cautiously towards Frederiksson.

'What's happened to you?' one of them enquired.

The thing merely continued its approach, teeth bared and the man with the rifle swiftly swung it up and shot the creature in the arm. It howled and turned to flee back down the tunnel.

'What the hell . . . ?' began the man tending Eriksson. 'Nils, why did you shoot him?'

'I've see that kind of thing before and I didn't act quickly enough then.' He turned to Eriksson. 'Is this Landsberg anything to do with that *thing*?'

'Yes, he . . . I don't know how, but that used to be one of our glaciologists, there are more and Landsberg claims to have made them like that.'

'Lars, Jon, keep watch all around us.' Nils looked at Eriksson. 'Tell me everything.'

It took only a few minutes for Eriksson to fill Nils in about the events of that night and the professor was grateful to be believed.

'You say that you've seen another wretch like that?' he asked.

'I've been in the mountain rescue service for fifteen years and there have been many disappearances in this area. Most were never seen again, dead or alive, but about five years ago I stumbled upon a body. It had been partially burned and I saw one of those things tearing at it, eating it. I stood frozen, then knew I must kill it or no one would ever believe me. I failed, it was faster than me and stronger — I chased it for a while to no avail and when I returned, the body was gone. From what you've told me, I think these freaks must have been attacking hikers for years, probably for that Landsberg to sacrifice.' He fell silent.

'I don't know if this frost giant of his is

pure delusion, although he may have found *something* strange, but he is definitely a murderer and he must be stopped before he kills anyone else.' Eriksson was feeling revived by this contact with decent, sane people and was fully resolved to eliminating Landsberg. 'Do you have any dynamite? We could collapse the entrance to that tunnel.'

'A small amount for clearing landslides, but I'd need to get inside that cavern. I want to see exactly what's going on there.' Nils grinned wryly. 'For all I know, you could be the villain and Landsberg the victim.'

'True enough,' Eriksson answered with a rare smile. 'I'll wait here where your friends can keep me under surveillance. But if you agree that we should do our best to take Landsberg out I want to help. We'll see just how much the bastard knows about my war record.'

★   ★   ★

Nils took a flare gun with him down the tunnel while Eriksson, Jon and Lars kept watch at the entrance. The two younger men had been horrified to hear the professor's tale and their leader's corroboration. If Nils had not returned in half an hour, they were to drive back to the research camp, calling for back-up on the way. As Nils had reasoned, even if no one were to believe the stranger facts, there was the body of Larsen to prove to police that something needed investigating.

After twenty minutes, Jon raised the rifle to his eye and took aim as they saw a figure emerging from the tunnel. Only when the figure had removed his hood and they could see Nils did he lower the gun.

'What did you see?'

'Things I hope one day to forget. Keep watching the tunnel. I don't think I was followed but we can't take the chance.'

'But, what was happening down there?' Eriksson urged. 'Why has nothing tried to come and drag me back?'

'I'd say that Landsberg's been a bit busy. You must have hit him with one of your shots. It looks like he's been patching up a wound on his leg and none of his monsters can be of help. I could see that those ghouls you described are still working on the ice — I'd guess they can only follow orders — and your former colleagues had their own task.' Nils stopped and looked directly at Eriksson. 'They were piling wood at the base of what looked like a metal sculpture of a tree. I think they plan to burn you on a depiction of Yggdrasil — the sacred tree at the centre of the Norse cosmology.'

'Well, to hell with that!' Eriksson said explosively.

'Should we call the police now?' Lars asked worriedly.

'Definitely, but don't tell them everything or they'll waste time thinking you're mad. Just say that we've discovered two members of the scientific team, one of whom appears to have attacked and killed the others. They should come armed. When they get here they can see for themselves.'

It was then that the attack came.

The professor let out a cry as he saw three figures coming at speed out of the tunnel. Nils raised his rifle and shot one in the chest. Eriksson pulled the chisel out of his coat but hesitated, he could just recognise the two men who had been his colleagues. Then one of them lunged for him and he automatically swung the chisel up to block the creature's arm. Overcoming his unwillingness, he plunged the chisel into his attacker's chest. It collapsed in the snow with a horrible groan.

Nils wrestled the remaining horror to the ground but was struggling to keep it there. It twisted and bucked, snarling and snapping at him. 'I want to keep this one alive if possible,' he gasped, struggling to keep it down.

Lars came dashing over with a set of straps used for securing equipment. 'Good thinking. Did you get through to the police?' Nils asked as the two of them set about buckling the thing's arms to its side.

'Yes, they should be here in about an hour. Let's strap it to the jeep. Perhaps there's something that can be done for it.'

'I rather think the only service we can do for my old colleagues is to end their existence, but I agree that we should try,' Eriksson said.

When they had satisfied themselves that their captive could not escape, Nils voiced the thought that had also been worrying Eriksson. 'What do you think Landsberg will do when these do not return with you in tow?' he asked.

'He's always been stubborn, so I can't believe he'll give up. I've been half-expecting to see him coming out to get me himself. I'm not sure we can wait for the police to be honest.'

As if in answer to his fears, there came a high-pitched keening from the glacier. They winced at the sound, and saw that their captive was straining mightily against the straps that held it. Then it suddenly stopped and looked up at them. Its face changed, flowed into a different form. For a moment Eriksson saw Landsberg's features looking at him. The eyes flicked briefly over all of them and took in the bodies on the snow. Returning to Eriksson with a look of pure hatred the thing spoke, its voice that of Landsberg. 'You will not stop me. I cannot fail now.' Then the face changed once more back to the snarling, warped visage of the creature.

'Dear God, that's horrible!' exclaimed Nils.

'And if Landsberg can do this, then I'm very afraid that his frost giant may be true as well.' Eriksson felt sick as he forced the admission out. It went against all his beliefs but he could not deny what he had just seen and looking back with honesty, the patterns he saw in the ice *had* looked like a giant ribcage. 'I was a very good shot in my youth, so if you will lend me your rifle I should be able to get him even though I can only see out of one eye. I very much doubt if any of those . . . *creatures* can raise the dead or they wouldn't have needed Landsberg. I wouldn't mind some company though.'

★   ★   ★

After a brief debate, all four men entered the tunnel. There was no one in sight for the length of it and, as they reached the mouth of the cavern they could see why. All the remaining creatures had gathered round the image of Yggdrasil and seemed to be waiting for something. A moment later, a figure emerged from the smaller tunnel at the far end, the one that led directly to the chamber of frozen bones.

'It's him!' Eriksson hissed.

'Looks like he's bleeding.' Lars raised his binoculars then exclaimed.

Landsberg was walking, a little unsteadily towards the iron tree.

'Give me the rifle, quickly!' Eriksson's voice was urgent. 'He's decided to make himself the sacrifice!'

Landsberg was now climbing onto the blackened metal and they saw him motion to his slaves to light the pyre.

Nils swiftly unslung the rifle. 'Don't miss!'

Eriksson focussed all his attention on the tree with its human occupant. He had hit targets at this middle range many times in the past, and on several occasions those targets had been men. He hoped fervently that he was right and that Landsberg had to be burned to death to complete the ritual. Squinting down the sight, he saw his target in the crosshairs, then squeezed the trigger.

The shot reverberated round the icy chamber and all heads turned towards them. All but one. Eriksson's aim had been good. Landsberg slithered down and landed in the unlit pyre, a bloody bullet-hole though his head. The Yorvaskr degenerates started to wail, their voices hideous and the former members of the expedition team howled in anguish.

Without a single word, the four men turned and ran back up the tunnel, the hideous lamentations in their ears, gnawing at their very souls. Jon reached the entrance first and flicked open his lighter, hand poised over the explosive charge they had prepared. As Eriksson, bringing up the rear, emerged, he lit the fuse and hurled the charge down the tunnel. A few moments later there was a dull boom and a great rush of air as the tunnel collapsed, burying the one route out of the glacier, sealing in all of its inhabitants. Relief flooded through Eriksson, coupled with utter exhaustion and the sound of the approaching search and rescue helicopter was the most welcome thing he could imagine.

As it circled, looking for a place to land, Eriksson wondered briefly if anyone would believe them.

A quick glance at their grotesque captive, still strapped to the side of the jeep, reassured him on that point and he slumped back to wait gratefully for the helicopter.

★　★　★

Less than fifteen minutes later they were airborne, Eriksson having taken his position next to the pilot whilst the others kept an eye on the still struggling thing they had taken on board. Dawn was just breaking as the helicopter climbed higher, cresting the glacier and rising up into the heavens. It was then, as he looked down, that he saw in the early morning sunlight something that was to ensure that never again would he come out this way or doubt the old myths and legends.

For there, beneath the ice, he saw the shadowy impression of something gargantuan; something that spanned a huge portion of the mass of frozen ice just beyond where Landsberg's tunnel system ended — was it his imagination or did the contours of the glacier conform to the shape of a vast, six-mile long, coiled, serpentine outline that only disappeared from view as the helicopter veered away, back to civilisation?

Jormungandr!

3

CALLING ALL WEAKLINGS!

You too can have a body like mine!

'*Stand up for yourself, Sam! What are you, a man or a mouse? You always were a sickly child. You're too weak. Get some muscles. Eat your greens like Doctor Metcalfe told you to.*' Sam Perkins' mother — Edith Perkins — was nagging at him again, berating him, screeching like a harpy, her words cutting him to the bone even though she had been dead for over four years.

Perkins mumbled something in his sleep, gripping his pillow.

'*You're nothing but a weakling, Sam!*' his mother taunted. '*A big drip! The kids at school were right to bully you. Back then you were just a wimp. Back then there was more meat on a butcher's pencil! Now look at you! You've gone* from one extreme to the other. *You're just a quivering mound of fat! A lazy, slothful, good-for-nothing tub of lard!'*

Perkins' groans became louder as he tried to battle his way free from his nightmare.

'You're nothing but a big cry-baby. Look at you! A feeble excuse for a man,' Edith spat venomously. *'All your life you've let people walk all over you. It's no wonder you've never had a girlfriend.'*

'Mnnn. Lemme alone . . . ' Perkins was quivering. A trickle of saliva drooled from the corner of his mouth. His flabby body was slick with damp, cold sweat. Fat, fleshy fingers clenched and unclenched his blanket.

'You've gone from a skinny whelp to a slovenly pig. It's no wonder everyone makes fun of you and talks behind your back,' his dead mother cried. *'There's not an ounce of muscle on you. Just fat. You'll never get a wife or a proper job.'*

'Mother — '

'Don't you Mother me, you disgusting slob.'

Jowls wobbling, Perkins savagely shook

his head from side to side in an attempt to shake off the nightmare. Wide-eyed, he stared blindly around him trying to make out forms in the shadow-filled darkness. The terrible, recurring dream was still fresh in his brain, the images of his senile and vindictive mother with her wagging finger, lodged indelibly in his mind. With great heaving breaths, he reached over to one side and switched on the bedside lamp.

Edith Perkins, her blue-rinsed hair, thick NHS glasses and ill-fitting false teeth, was sat in her wheelchair at the edge of the bed.

A muffled shriek left his lips as he jerked awake properly this time. Reaching shakily for his glasses, he scanned his empty bedroom.

★   ★   ★

'For God's sake, Perkins. I've told you before not to eat in the post-room. Look, you're getting greasy fingerprints all over the envelopes! Hell, you had lunch only an hour ago.'

Perkins looked guiltily at his boss, seeing the barely concealed contempt on Mr. Enfield's face. 'Sorry sir.'

'Oh, just get on with the post, and bin that pork pie.' Mr. Enfield left, shaking his head in mixed disbelief and anger.

With one eye on the door, Perkins slowly finished the pie and wiped his greasy hands on his trousers. Sorting the post was a boring, mindless task and it suited him down to the ground, except for the unwelcome interruptions from his boss. His job was officially titled, Junior Clerk, but he had been there six years and everyone still called him 'the post-boy', despite the fact that he was thirty-two years old.

At half-past one, Perkins took the sack of stamped mail to the post office at the end of the road as usual and slouched back to his small room with two packets of crisps tucked under his jumper and a bar of chocolate in his back pocket. As he passed the tearoom, he overheard Mr. Enfield saying his name and paused to listen.

'That Perkins, I'm sure there's something wrong with him. I mean, the blank looks he gives you, it's like there's no one home most of the time and I'm sure I've heard him talking to himself.'

'And he's so fat and flabby. That can't be healthy. I'd say something, encourage him to slim down a bit, but to be honest he scares me.' That was Mrs. Siddenham, head typist and a self-righteous gossip who was as lean as a rake and famously never let a biscuit pass her lips. 'Can't you do something, Mr. Enfield? Get him transferred to the Bolton office or something?' The wheedling tone of her voice sickened Perkins and the reply from his boss wasn't much better.

'Don't think the thought hasn't crossed my mind but, no, they already have enough retards up there at the moment. We're stuck with him, unless he really screws up of course. The only reason I gave him this job is because I used to know his old man, back in my army days. A fine fellow. Honestly, if Perkins senior could see his son now he'd be disgusted.'

'I agree. He's an absolute disgrace,' Mr. Travis, the stock-controller added. 'He spends more time eating than he does

116

working. I'd have thought that would be enough for Head Office to give him the boot. He smells as well.'

Perkins felt sick. He was trembling all over with hard-to-contain rage. He heard one of them rise from their chair and so he turned and quickly made his way to the toilets. On legs that felt as though they had turned to jelly, he went into one of the cubicles, locked the door and sat on the lavatory, his head in his hands. He had always known that his colleagues didn't think that much of him but to have overheard the things they had said —

'*I told you they talked about you.*' His mother's acerbic words struck him like a splash of battery acid. '*It's all they do. It was the same at school. Look! Here's Skinny Perkins! Here's Skinny Perkins!*' She repeatedly chanted the childish nickname at him.

'Stop! Please stop!' Perkins whimpered.

'*Here's Skinny Perkins. Although it's not Skinny Perkins any more, is it? Not even Puny Perkins. No! It's Fatty Perkins now, isn't it? Here's Fatty Perkins! Here's Fatty Perkins . . .* '

'Leave me alone,' he whispered through gritted teeth. He sat on the toilet for a further twenty minutes before returning to work, the insane, incessant, torturing taunts from his mother beginning to gradually fade away.

★   ★   ★

The day finally ended and Perkins caught his bus home. The bus was cramped but he usually managed to get a seat to himself, as there was not much room for another person and besides it seemed that people would rather stand than sit next to him. He was conscious of the judge-mental glances of his fellow passengers and the snide comments made by some — or was that inside his head? Whatever the case, he was thankful when the journey ended and the bus debouched him close to his house.

The grey, terraced building — a classic two up, two down — was cold, empty and uninviting as usual. The garden lay untidy and neglected. Opening the front door, he draped his jacket over the banister and headed for the kitchen to make himself a snack. Clearing the table by shoving yesterday's detritus off the other end, he assembled a sandwich and sat in silence to eat, the hurtful voices in his head mercifully quiet for the moment.

As usual at six o'clock he turned on his radio and listened to the news with no particular interest. He knew that by the end of the news the local chip shop would be open and his daily order of two steak and kidney puddings, chips and a large bottle of cream soda would be wrapped and ready for him to collect. At least Mrs. Bennet, the lady in the chip shop was happy to see him each evening. She had known him since the skinny days and always had a smile and a kind word for him.

With the ending of the last bulletin, Perkins pulled himself to his feet and headed out for his supper. It was a relatively short distance but he was so out of shape that it took him the best part of ten minutes to get there. Puffing and red-faced, he entered the chip shop.

'Hello love. One of the fryers has been

playing up so it'll be another fifteen minutes or so for your chips.' Mrs. Bennet gestured to one of the empty chairs. 'Take a seat.'

'That's alright Mrs. B.' Perkins sat down, happily inhaling the welcoming and familiar scents of deep-fried food, salt and vinegar that wafted from behind the counter. Throughout his unhappy upbringing, and his years of being bullied both as a child and as an adult, he had always found this place a refuge of sorts. Idly, he reached for a magazine.

Several minutes later the door was pushed open and three loud-mouths came in, smelling of beer. Perkins' heart sank. Right now he wanted to melt away, to surreptitiously vanish from sight.

'Three cod and chips and make it snappy,' one called loudly as the other two leant on the counter, their scruffy overalls and heavy-duty boots grimy with dirt from the factory nearby.

Perkins shrunk back behind his raised magazine and prayed not to be noticed. Just a few minutes and they would be gone. If only he could remain inconspicuous —

'Oi, I know you, don't I?' A grubby hand roughly forced the magazine down.

'D . . . do you?' Perkins mumbled, looking away.

'Yeah, I used to go to school with you. You're Perkins.' The man belched, his foul beery breath making Perkins wince. 'You were a skinny freak, weren't you?' The ruffian's voice became more belligerent. 'I remember you. Bloody hell guys,' he said, addressing his cronies. 'Bet none of you can believe this bloater used to be the skinniest kid in school.'

'Well, he's certainly made up for it!' replied one of the others.

'Too right, he has.' The bully gave Perkins an unfriendly slap on his belly, chortling to himself. 'Remember me, Tony Jaggers?'

Perkins mumbled something non-committal but yes, he remembered Jaggers alright. A right bad egg. A mean-hearted lout who was only happy when he was ridiculing others. It appeared that this schoolyard bully hadn't changed at all. The years had, if anything, made him worse.

'Better watch that chair don't break

under you,' laughed one of Jaggers' mates.

'I hope we're served before he buys the bloody shop out,' commented the other man.

At that moment Mrs. Bennet came back with three wrapped parcels and eyes like flint. 'Three cod and chips,' she said, dumping them down on the counter.

'Better watch this one missus, he'll eat the bloody shop!' the old school 'mate' called jeeringly, gathering up his cod and chips.

Mrs. Bennett turned red and leant over the counter. 'You should be ashamed of yourselves. I've barred customers before for pestering folk like that but they were all kids. Call yourselves men! I know you Tony Jaggers. You've always been a bad 'un, just like your old man before you.'

'Keep your bloody hair on you old bat. I'm just having a bit of fun with an old school pal!' Jaggers grinned and reached out to ruffle Perkins' hair jeeringly. 'Ain't that right, Fatty?'

Perkins cringed away from the hand, a learned response from many years ago.

God alone knew how many times he had been on the receiving end of Tony Jagger's and his gang's abuse. In a sudden flash of memory, he remembered his first day at school. He saw Jaggers and some of his friends pointing and laughing at him, having thrown his P.E. kit on top of the bike shed, well out of reach. A large crowd had gathered round that day to laugh and point; almost every kid in the school, all intent on making his life one long misery, all knowing that Mr. Blake, the P.E. instructor, forced those kids who didn't have their kit to exercise in their underpants. The humiliating experience had reduced him to tears. His torment had gone on for years. In many ways it had never ended. Adulthood had only made the bullying verbal and emotional as opposed to physical but if he didn't watch what he did then things could soon change. In his mind's eye, he envisaged Jaggers and his mates waiting for him outside in order to beat him up.

'Be off with you before I call the police!' shouted Mrs. Bennet.

Jaggers took a bite of one of his chips

and then spat it out. 'They're bloody freezing.' Angrily, he threw the bag to the floor at Perkins' feet. 'Hell, no doubt you'll still eat 'em.' He turned to the others. 'Come on, let's go. It stinks in here and the last thing I want is for Fatty here to wet himself like he used to do at school. Besides, the grub's rubbish.'

Cursing, the three of them stormed out and slammed the door.

'Are you alright, dearie?' asked Mrs. Bennet worriedly.

There was a tightness in Perkins' stomach and a dim fuzziness in his brain. He looked at his right hand, which still grasped the magazine and was surprised to see that it was shaking. He was only vaguely aware that the chip shop owner was talking to him for he was so lost in the thoughts of yesteryear; the daily beatings and the constant, never-ending harassment.

'*I told you, Sam. You're just a big, blubbing girl.*' His mother, that old battleaxe, was back, invading his private thoughts without a care. '*Now a real man would go out there and give that Tony*

Jaggers and his pals what for. But you're a coward, aren't you? A big girl's blouse. You couldn't fight your way out of a wet paper bag. I've scraped sterner things off the base of my shoes.'

'Please, Mother — '

'Eh? What's that, love?' queried Mrs. Bennet.

Perkins jerked back into reality. 'Oh, nothing.' He saw the plastic bag resting atop the counter. 'Is that my order?'

'Yes. Now, don't you go letting those three wastrels upset you.'

'Don't worry about that. I've had to put up with the likes of Tony Jaggers all my life.' Perkins grabbed the bag. With a nod of thanks, he morosely left the chip shop and started on the short trudge home.

He had only been going about five minutes when he saw his three tormentors sauntering towards him. Gulping nervously, he turned his head to see if there was anyone in sight, a helpful policeman for instance. There was nobody bar a few kids out playing football way back just outside the chip shop he had recently left. For a moment, he considered retracing his steps and walking back the way he had come in order to take a diversion down one of the other roads in an attempt to evade them but his heart sank when he realised that they had seen him and that no matter what he did they were bound to catch up with him. He prepared himself for the inevitable. He could only hope that they'd make whatever they were going to do to him quick and that they would limit their bullying to the purely verbal. One on one he thought he might have been able to handle himself but not against three. But that was it with bullies, wasn't it? They never acted alone, lacking the courage to confront their victim fairly.

Jaggers walked up and started to jog on the spot, his movements exaggerated. 'I was going to go for my evening run. I don't know which'll take longer; once round you or twice around the gasworks.'

That won a round of harsh laughter from his mates.

'Stop bothering me, will you?' said Perkins quaveringly. Blood was coursing through his veins and a knot of sick fear had tightened in the pit of his stomach. Whilst he doubted that the three of them would go as far as to assault him in the middle of the street their cruel actions were still giving him cause for concern. With a gulp, he tried to push past, to resume his homeward journey.

'Watch where you're going, would you?' said one of Jagger's friends, stepping aside.

Head down and muttering darkly to himself, Perkins kept walking. With each forward step he was shortening the distance to his house.

The bullies harried his every move, their taunts and barbed comments all aimed at trying to provoke a reaction. But if there was one thing that Perkins had managed to do over the years it was to harden himself to the victimisation; inuring himself against the remarks of others even though by now his mother was getting in on the act. The old harridan was forever pecking at him with her vitriolic and scathing words, reinforcing everything that Jaggers and the others were saying.

Still Perkins plodded on, occasionally having to step around one of the three men as they tried to repeatedly block his path. It was this stoic refusal to rise to the intimidation that finally caused Jaggers to resort to physical contact. Sticking out his boot, he tripped his victim up, sending him sprawling on the pavement. The cream soda bottle in the bag smashed.

Jaggers' mates laughed.

Perkins lay there, too shocked and surprised at the moment to feel any hurt. Then pain did register in his numbed body from where he had landed on his left knee. His palms were grazed and bleeding. Through tearful eyes, he looked up and for a time he was a little, skinny boy once more, lying on the school playground after one of many beatings, his nose a squashed tomato dripping blood, his glasses lying nearby. On some occasions in the past, he was sure they had intended to kill him not just 'teach him a lesson'.

'*Like I keep telling you. You're nothing but a sissy. You're a wimp!*' Edith was back to her spiteful bitching. '*You hear me? You're just a wimp!'*

'Go away, Mother. Just go away. I don't want you telling me — ' Perkins began burbling through trembling lips.

'What's he on about?' asked one of Jagger's pals. 'I think he thinks you're his mother. Blimey, you didn't say he was nuts as well as fat.'

'Crazy freak!' snarled Jaggers. He was tempted to give the man on the ground a kick but instead picked up the dropped bag and emptied the contents all over him. Their fun over for the evening they began laughing like retarded hyenas before heading off. If Perkins were to go home and call the police they'd just say that he tripped up. And it would be Fatty's word against theirs.

Now that they had gone, Perkins got to his feet, brushed off the offending chips and ruptured steak and kidney puddings, retrieved his glasses and limped the remaining distance to his house. With a deep sigh of relief, he got inside and shut the front door behind him. He wasn't that badly hurt — at least not physically, but he felt so humiliated and angry. He was angry at Jaggers and the others but deep down, he was more angry at himself. Everything they had all said, including his departed mother, was true. He was a coward. An overweight, whimpering coward, nothing more than an easy victim. It was almost as though he had been born with a sign around his neck that invited others to humiliate and bully him.

Gingerly, he rubbed his knee. No doubt it would soon swell up like a balloon. Wincing at the discomfort, he made his way upstairs and went into the bathroom. He switched on the light and moved towards the small mirror-fronted cabinet in order to get the first-aid box and some plasters. Catching sight of his own reflection he stopped short.

His mother had often told him to take a good look at himself, so that's exactly what he did. It was not long before he broke down in a flood of tears.

★   ★   ★

Perkins was up early the next morning. His night had thankfully been a relatively tranquil one, without any interruptions from his deceased, demanding mother. Maybe she was content that he had suffered enough the previous evening. No doubt it would only be a matter of time before she started up again.

His knee wasn't half as bad as he had envisaged it would have been. Once dressed, he went over to the window and threw wide the curtains. The street below was empty and quiet. In the grey morning light everything looked drab and depressing. He turned away from the window, opened his bedroom door and stepped out into the dimly-lit corridor beyond. The door directly in front of him led to the bathroom. The one to his right, at the end of the short corridor, led to his dead mother's bedroom. To his left, there was the landing and the stairs down to the hall.

He was just about to enter the bathroom when there came a loud crash from the room at the end of the corridor.

Perkins jumped. His nerves were afire.

Slowly, he made his way forward.

He paused outside, listening.

Twenty seconds passed. Silence.

With a trembling hand, he reached out for the handle, fingers circling the cold metal. He had not been inside this room for years. Three, maybe four years. He opened the door.

The door opened readily. The room beyond was much as he remembered it. A little dustier without doubt and there was a distinct mustiness in the air. Cobwebs had grown from the lights and a huge one had developed in the near corner above the bed. Standing at the threshold, he scanned the room, searching to see what had fallen and made the noise. His eyes settled on a painting, which had clearly slipped from the wall, its nail having come loose.

Mustering his albeit limited courage, Perkins went in and bent down in order to retrieve the painting. It was then that he noticed the white box under the bed. Curious, he edged forward, got down lower, reached under and pulled it out, eyes widening as he saw its contents.

It was crammed full of some of his old Science Fiction and Horror comics, books and magazines. Pleased with his find, he lifted the box on to the bed and began leafing through some of them. A smile creased his face as he noted the pre-decimalisation prices, the garish covers and such corny titles as; *Attack of the Bee Man, Satan's Mother, The Jelly from Hell* and *It Seeped from Beyond Uranus*. He remembered reading that one as a kid, oblivious to the innuendo.

Then he saw it. On crumbling, yellowed with age page thirty-seven of *The Jelly from Hell* opposite the page advertising *Joan the Wad, How to Win the Pools* and cures for varicose veins, ulcers, eczema and psoriasis:

CALLING ALL WEAKLINGS!

YOU TOO CAN HAVE A BODY LIKE MINE!

Beneath this audacious claim there was a grainy black and white photograph of a grinning, trunk-wearing, muscle-bound Hercules, one arm raised in order to show off his enlarged biceps.

Leonard Maximus. That was the name of the he-man. It was all coming back to Perkins now. He remembered as a boy how he had once scrounged some money from an aunt — there was no way his mother would have funded such daftness — and secretly written off for the details of how to obtain such a statuesque physique. It had promised so much to a skinny and often bullied kid; gaining muscle and enhanced energy. He had received a small booklet with exercises and dietary advice but his mother had soon discovered it and made him send it back for a refund, calling it a waste of money.

Now, almost twenty years later, he found himself drawn to the advertisement once again. So much of it was in tiny, barely readable print that he had to search around in one of the nearby cabinets for his mother's old magnifying glass before he could make it out. Reading the extraordinary claims for transformation he chuckled at first and was about to put the book back when he glanced across at the mirror on the dressing table. His reflection looked even worse than the previous night and he suddenly wondered what he might have been like had the exercise course been any good. What if he had persevered with it, how might his life have been different? From that thought it was but a short leap to the question — could his life still be transformed?

Perkins checked the address at the bottom of the advertisement: *28 Deans Road, Nottingham*. A faint hope began to grow within him. Was it possible, after all these years that the firm that made such products would still be going? Could he truly make a difference, even now?

And what of Mr. Maximus himself? What had become of him? Did he even exist or was the photograph just of some generic bodybuilder used to promote what, in essence, was probably nothing more than a cheap commercial gimmick? '*You too can have a body like mine*'. Hell, in the small print there was even a money back guarantee if the buyer was not fully satisfied with the product.

Perkins grinned cynically at the thought that Mr. Maximus — assuming that he was a real person and that he was still alive — must be in his late fifties, possibly even in his sixties by now. The last thing he wanted was the body of an old man with wasted muscles and a beer belly.

As he sat there a sudden and unaccustomed resolve came to him. He had to start making changes in his life so why not begin here, or with something similar? After all, nothing ventured, nothing gained. He guessed that about three decimal pounds would equate to the original price and, before he could change his mind, he stuffed the book into his pocket. He would pinch an envelope and stamp from work and send the coupon off from there.

*　*　*

Two weeks had gone past — two weeks of growing tension at work as he overheard with increasing frequency the negative and nasty backchat about him. In addition, Edith stepped up her verbal assault inside his mind, incessantly going on and on at him — highlighting his physical and emotional failings and repeatedly informing him how bad an opinion others had of him. Consequently, he had entirely forgotten all about Leonard Maximus and his stupendous claims.

Thus it came as quite a surprise when he returned home one evening — an evening in which he had got soaked after having to wait for a later bus, having seen Jaggers sat inside his usual one; still he had picked up his chip shop supper on the way back — to find a parcel waiting for him. For a moment he stood there puzzled, unsure as to what it might be. Then he noticed the return address: *28 Deans Road, Nottingham*.

With a buzz of excitement, he took his supper and the parcel into the kitchen, and rested the lot on the table. He opened the parcel. Inside there was a familiar small instruction booklet, which contained various daily exercises, stretches and dietary advice. It was the exact same. He had expected something a bit glossier this time, more modern but this could even have been the very one his mother had forced him to return. There was a typed sheet of paper with the same 1950s photograph of Mr. Maximus below which were a few paragraphs thanking him for buying the product as well as extolling the virtues it could impart.

Greedily tucking in to the first of his steak and kidney puddings, he began to read. After a while, he looked appraisingly at the second pudding and with a great effort of will wrapped it up and threw it in the bin.

* * *

The following day was a Saturday. With a groan, Perkins shoved his mother's old bed to the edge of the room and began clearing the rest of the furniture in order to make himself an exercise space. Part of him wasn't all that happy about being in here but there was nowhere else in the house that was suitable. His own bedroom was too small and the last thing he wanted was someone walking by the house to see him puffing and panting embarrassingly. No, it had to be upstairs.

The booklet instructed that only ten minutes a day of exercise was required. Perkins believed he could probably handle this. After all, what was ten minutes — it was the same amount of time it took him to walk to the chip shop. Opening the booklet to page one, he studied the various drawings and poses therein and began to duplicate them. Some of the stretches he found difficult and there was no way on earth that he was going to be able to touch his toes, never mind complete thirty sit-ups and twenty press-ups. That level of exercise would have to wait until much later. Nevertheless, he succeeded in doing most of what was needed.

After the ten minutes was up, with a small sense of achievement, and a stiffness and ache in his body, Perkins got to his feet with the help of the bed. He felt pleased that he had made a start and that the exercises hadn't been too difficult. He would have to alter his diet quite drastically but that was a price he was prepared to pay. It would be hard. No doubt about that, harder perhaps than the actual physical exercise but the important thing was he felt he could do it.

'*Oh no you can't. Don't even think it.*

You'll be back on the puddings in no time. Mark my words, Sam. You'll give it up within a week and be even fatter.'

'No, not this time, Mother. I'm going to be like Mr. Maximus. I've heard enough from you.'

'Don't you talk to me like that!'

'Mother, shut up!'

And for once his mother did.

* * *

The days turned into weeks and faithfully and rigorously Perkins kept up with his daily exercises. The stretching and the few muscle-building routines gradually became easier and for the main part he stuck to his new eating programme. He received only one visitor during that time — Mrs. Bennet, the chip shop owner who had become concerned about his lack of custom.

He had now completed Stage One.

Appraising himself in the mirror in the hall, he thought he looked a bit trimmer around the face and stomach and there was more of a spring in his step but he was a long way from having a truly muscled body like Mr. Maximus. He could lift more and he could now do several push-ups but there was still an observable flabbiness to him. Without access to a set of scales he had no idea of his weight, but he had read in the guide book that muscle was heavier than fat so presumably he hadn't lost that much. Perhaps he had even put weight on despite having drastically curtailed his junk food intake.

Stage Two of the programme arrived. This was a little more intense and some of the exercise routines seemed, certainly to Perkins' mind, to border on the outlandish. The postures and the various stances which he was instructed to maintain for up to a minute at a time were truly bizarre; such as standing on one leg with both arms extended or attempting to sit cross-legged with his hands held as though in prayer in front of his face. There was a greater emphasis on protein intake in his diet, including lightly steamed liver, which he was not too keen on, but he was managing.

The best thing was that when he was

exercising he didn't hear his mother.

For ten minutes each day he enjoyed the silence of his own thoughts and felt a numb sort of calmness inside. That alone kept him on track for another two weeks of strange food and stranger work. One of his exercises was almost like a dance with precise movements that the booklet said promoted balance and strength. Wobbling slightly as he went through the motions, Perkins was reminded one day of a martial arts film he had seen. Perhaps he could take up something like that once he was fit. His mind drifted to the point at which he toppled over with a resounding thud.

After two months, Perkins completed Stage Two. He was finding the exercises easier and had made big strides with his food but he was feeling fed up. The promised transformation wasn't really happening. Yes, he was better than he had been, but the lofty claims of the advertisement and the booklets had not materialised and he was running out of patience. His stomach was less tubby but he wanted a torso rippling with muscles that the women would adore; washboard abdominals, legs like tree trunks and flexed biceps that could crush walnuts. He wanted to be able to tear telephone directories in half with his bare hands and —

Get revenge? Was that the driving force behind everything? Is that what he really desired? Did he want to get his own back on those that had tormented him, make them pay for years of suffering? He wasn't sure. Certainly he had never considered himself a vengeful person. All he wanted was to be able to stick up for himself and ensure that no one started on him in the first place. With a body like Mr. Maximus surely no one would dare.

One evening, while doing the ten push-ups that he could now complete, a memory came to him, *'satisfaction guaranteed or your money back'*. Well, he wasn't satisfied yet so maybe he should get his money back. Although, to be honest, he didn't want the money, he wanted it to work. Switching over to the almost meditative section of his workout, he wondered what he should do. As the familiar calming effect of the slow movements washed over him he made up his mind. He would write to the company and put it to them. Perhaps he was doing something wrong, something that Mr. Maximus, or whoever his representative was, could put right, and if not then maybe he should get refunded and he could go and buy some dumbbells, take up swimming or something. Happy with his decision, Perkins continued to trace the archaic patterns in the air with his hands and feet, oblivious to the fact that this mental and physical training was now taking closer to an hour of his time each day.

* * *

The next morning, letter of dissatisfaction in hand, Perkins was just about to head out when there came a loud knock at the front door. Opening it, he was confronted by the postman who handed over a brown paper package.

'Delivery for Mr. S. Perkins.'

'Thanks.' Perkins took the package,

closed the door and went into the kitchen.

Avidly, he opened it up. Inside was a booklet labelled *Stage Three*, a signed, framed photograph of Mr. Maximus and a small plastic vial of clear liquid encased in bubble wrap. He glanced at the photograph before picking up the booklet and turning to the front page expecting to see more diagrammatic postures and instructions. Instead there was but one word: *DRINK*.

He stared at it. Was it an instruction? For some reason it seemed more like a command. Confused, he flipped the booklet over to see if there was anything else. But this was absurd, he thought, his eyes now turning to the bottle of fluid.

So it had all been a scam after all! No doubt this two-bit, phony operation had duped countless gullible individuals like himself into parting with their cash for a long time. It was just the same as all of those other advertisements that promised so much; such as the lucky Cornish piskey that brought wealth and fortune, the treatment for varicose veins or the guaranteed means to give up smoking. It was all fake. Absolute nonsense. No doubt he would get no reply to his letter of complaint.

His eyes were drawn to the bottle.

'I told you it were a waste of money, didn't I? All that money for some cheap pamphlets and a bottle of tap water. I bet that Maximus crook is laughing at you even now' For the first time in weeks his mother returned, her words as caustic as ever. *'You've been taken for a mug. Pah! All that dancing and cavorting you've been doing in my bedroom. At times you've looked like a right pansy. A ballerina. In a week's time you'll have undone all that work you did and you'll have slipped back into your old ways, sitting at the kitchen table munching your chips and eating your steak and kidney puddings, piling on the lard.'*

DRINK.

Perkins ripped the bottle from its wrapping. He examined it. Turned it upside down and gave it a shake. It was still and unremarkable. It certainly had the appearance of nothing more spectacular than

146

plain old tap water.

'*That's because that's all it is*' croaked Edith. '*You think it's some kind of miracle tonic, don't you? Well go on then, drink it!*'

Carefully unscrewing the cap, Perkins gave it a sniff. The last thing he wanted was for him to have accidentally been sent some other product — a treatment for baldness for example — and for him to drink it by mistake.

'Ah well, here goes.' He raised it to his lips and drank it down in one long gulp.

It tasted unlike anything he had ever drunk before. There was a slight sharpness to it; a mild bitterness that lingered as a rather unpleasant aftertaste, which made him wince. He doubted whether it was water, even given the possibility that it had been flavoured with some form of additive. His lips and tongue felt dry.

He put the empty bottle down.

To his amazement, he noticed that the instruction in the book had changed. It now read: *SLEEP*.

Straightening his glasses, Perkins looked at the page. He picked the booklet up.

Walking over to the window, he held it up to see if there was any kind of residual image of the word that had been there before in the belief that this change may have been down to some kind of invisible ink trickery. There was nothing. Just the new word.

The strange thing was, despite having been awake less than an hour and the fact that he had work to go to, he did feel tired. Was it because of the mysterious drink he had just imbibed — or was it due to the suggestive power of the instruction?

This was a form of weariness he had never experienced before. It was a battle to keep his eyes open. His mind was wandering. Unsteadily, Perkins reached the kitchen door and walked like a somnambulist to the foot of the stairs. The sense of lethargy and drowsiness almost made him fall asleep right there in the hall. From somewhere, he got the strength to crawl up the stairs to his bedroom, that sensation that someone had secured a great weight around his neck making his movements very slow.

Lacking the energy to get undressed, he just slumped down onto his bed. He was soon fast asleep.

* * *

'*Wake up, Sam! Get out of your bed! There's someone prowling around!*' Edith sounded unusually scared.

Perkins had no idea where he was. There seemed to be no form to his surroundings, nothing tangible to grasp hold of. Even his mother's voice was faint. Turning round, he saw a dim shape, possibly that of a man but he couldn't be sure.

'Mother? What's happening?' he called out.

'*There's someone else in here, I tell you. You've let him in! You always were a fool.*' Her voice was growing weaker and weaker. The last words came to him as just a whisper. Then she was gone. He felt an absolute certainty about that. But he did not feel alone.

'Who's there?' he quavered.

'Why, it's me of course.' A firm voice answered. 'You called for me, remember?'

The shape grew nearer and Perkins gradually made out the familiar face of Leonard Maximus.

'Am I dreaming?' he asked, trying to control his nervous voice.

'In a way.' Maximus smiled broadly at him. 'Don't worry, it won't last long. You did everything right.'

'Have I finished the course then? Will I be like you now?' Hope began to grow in him, despite his wariness.

'Yes, just like me, lad. Tell me, what would you really like to do with your new body?' Maximus seemed so friendly, almost paternal, that Perkins answered immediately and straight from the heart.

'I'd like to show that bastard, Jaggers. Then . . . well, I'm not sure. There's so much I could do.'

'I'll bear that in mind.' Maximus was very close to Perkins now. 'For the moment though you should sleep. Just let go. I'll look after things.'

Perkins found he could not disobey, nor did he want to. It would be alright, he just had to let Mr. Maximus be in charge. All would be fine.

Opening his eyes, he reached for his glasses out of habit. Putting them on, he blinked at the fuzzy image before remembering that he didn't need them. He sat up and looked round at the small, dreary room. He had not seen it before but it was the usual kind of pathetic reflection of his host that he was used to. Now to business.

The clothes he was wearing were no good, too loose in some places, too tight in others. Concentrating briefly, he closed his eyes and when he re-opened them his preferred outfit was there. Much better. Energetically bounding down the stairs, he swung into the kitchen and found what he was looking for. On the table was an empty bottle and a photograph. Now to check it had worked. The photograph showed a fat, sad-looking man with thick glasses. It was signed: *Samuel Perkins*.

Leonard Maximus nodded with satisfaction and then watched as the photograph burst into flames. Now on to the next task . . .

Tony Jaggers was leafing through the local paper over his lunch when his eyes fell upon a certain face. *Local man missing. Police searching the canal* read the caption underneath Sam Perkins' picture.

'Well I'll be . . . Hey, Joe! Looks like my old mate Perkins has topped himself!' He called out to one of his cronies. 'Wouldn't have thought he'd have the guts.' Jaggers read the article for a few seconds more, then lost interest and turned the page.

It was only later that Perkins was brought back to his mind. Walking home from the bus stop he heard someone whistling behind him and then felt a steely grip on his shoulder.

'Hello Tony. Remember me?'

Jaggers spun round, recognising the menace in the voice, although the lantern-jawed man in front of him was a dark-coated stranger. His first thought was to be menacing in return but the stranger was taller and undoubtedly stronger than him. Hell, the guy looked like Johnny Weismüller's bigger brother!

'Don't think I do, mate.' Jaggers tried to answer jovially but his heart was starting to pound. There was something about this situation that was making alarm bells ring in his head.

'Come now, Tony. All those years of bullying poor Sam Perkins. The taunts, the blows, the casual torture. You recognised him alright in the chip shop that time, even though he had changed since his schooldays, filled out a bit you might say.' Maximus was slowly backing Jaggers up a small alleyway as he talked.

'Perkins! He . . . I read he's vanished. You're not Perkins so don't mess about.' Jaggers stumbled but righted himself. He started to prepare himself up for the fight he could see was coming.

'Oh, but I am. All that is left of Sam Perkins is here inside me.' The stranger grinned and tapped his head. 'He called me in you see, to sort his life out. He'll never be a target again, never be hurt or humiliated by the likes of you.'

Maximus was sneering now, but Jaggers was more frightened by the ghost of a face that he could see overlaid on the

153

muscleman's features. It *was* Perkins for a moment, both the skinny boy and the overweight man. Then the image receded.

'Get away from me!' Jaggers yelled and scooped up a discarded bottle, swinging it at Maximus' face but missing.

'Can't do that, Tony. I have a task to fulfil, a truly satisfying one I might add.' He closed in on Jaggers, easily grabbing the other by the wrist and shaking the bottle from him. 'I owe Perkins that. All my little lads get what I promise if they're good, namely a body like mine. It's all in the contract, you see. It's stated quite clearly in the small print. Pity it's too small for most to read but, hey, it's there none the less. In return, I get everything that they were or could've been.'

'No! Get away!' Jaggers was pleading now. Feebly, he raised an arm to try and ward off any attack.

'Really? Is that your best? A big tough man like you?' Maximus smiled. 'You ever heard of the phrase 'those who live by the sword, die by the sword', Tony? No? Well, let me show you. Don't worry. It should only hurt for an eternity.' With a vice-like grip, he grabbed Jaggers around the throat and raised him, one-handed, off the ground. He held him there, squeezing, until his victim's legs had stopped kicking and his face had turned blue before dropping him to the cobbles.

Sauntering out of the alley, Maximus straightened his collar, brushed off his cuffs and smoothed back his perfect hair. The sensation of life was as intoxicating and addictive as ever and the new addition to his collection of souls was proving to be a good one. Poor old Fatty Perkins was rich pickings for a demon such as him. So much stored up resentment, so many scores to settle, so much *fun* to be had in avenging his hurts. It would be easy to delve into the psyche of the one he now inhabited, ransack through the tortured memories. There were others on the list. Others to whom payback was long overdue.

'*You filthy murderer!*' Maximus spun round at the hurled insult, but there was no one there. He was alone in the quickly darkening street.

'*You're a scumbag! Worse by far than*

my Sam. I'll make you pay!' The voice was loud in his ears but he couldn't work out where it was coming from. Trawling hurriedly through Perkins' memories, he matched the grating voice to an image — a wrinkled face, twisted with contempt, white-blue hair done up in curlers and thick glasses. But surely this old harpy was dead?

'*I swore I'd never leave him. The useless lump couldn't cope without me.'* Edith's voice was back. It was like invisible fingernails running down a blackboard inside his head. '*I'll hound you until you die. I can see now what you did to my boy; the godless rituals you called exercises, making the poor slob seal his own fate. Well I didn't do any of that prancing about. You can't force me out!'* She ended with an awful, insane cackle of malicious glee.

With a sick revulsion, the demon that was Maximus realised that in subsuming Sam Perkins he had got more than he had bargained for. A free gift, if you like.

The horrible, vicious, mad voice of Edith Perkins ranted at him as he held his head in his hands. Through the screeches and taunts he just managed to make out a faint whisper — *You too can have a mother like mine.*

4

PALE LILAC

*A stranger with a strange obsession
had come to Harvest Wood . . .*

It was a wet Tuesday evening and
Maggie's Bar was quiet, empty almost,
with only a few regulars and old-timers
inside. Some dull country and western
track was playing on the jukebox and in
the corner, near the bar, a black and
white television was showing a late-night
boxing match, the commentator failing to
arouse any kind of passion amongst the
handful of viewers inside.

Sheriff Rod Hooper was off-duty.
Peering along the length of his pool cue,
lining up his shot, he made a deft forward
thrust, cursing as the white ball missed
the remaining black.

'Looks like your luck's run out.'
Maggie Brennan, the owner of the bar,

screwed back and potted the eight-ball. 'Guess that'll be five bucks, sheriff.'

Hooper laughed. 'Ah well, maybe next time.' Returning his pool cue to the rack, he picked up his beer from a nearby table and took a swig. He delved into his pocket for the cash and handed it over.

'Do you want another game?'

'Just so as you can beat me again and show me up in front of all these . . . ' Hooper looked about him, wondering how exactly, and more to the point, politely, he could describe the uninterested aged patrons, ' . . . fine folk? Besides, I can't afford to play you anymore.' He turned to Maggie and smiled, liking what he saw. Thirty-three years old, auburn haired, bright blue eyes and one hell of a figure. Admittedly, she wasn't the brightest of women but she was by far the prettiest in town. He himself was in his mid-fifties with two divorces under his belt and a considerable belly above it.

'Suit yourself.' Maggie went behind the bar.

'Say, Maggie. You heard of anything

recently? Anything I need to know about?' This was something Hooper asked her every time he came in. It had become a routine. Like nearly everyone he knew, he had lived in Harvest Wood, the small town ten miles south of Crawford close to the Nebraska-Wyoming border, all of his life and he knew that all local gossip eventually filtered its way through to the bar. He found out about more things that were going on in here than he did on his police radio.

'I hear tell that Old Jed's dog died the other day. That damn mutt must've been nearly as old as he is.' Maggie began cleaning some of the glasses. 'Do you want another beer?'

'No, I'll just have this one and then that's me.'

'Suit yourself.' Maggie began stacking some of the glasses away. Suddenly she stopped and turned. 'Gee, I nearly forgot, but I don't suppose you've heard the news about Aubrey?'

'Aubrey? Aubrey Penton?'

'Yeah. Seems that he's managed to shift the old MacPherson place.'

Hooper raised his eyebrows in surprise. 'God, I didn't think anybody would ever buy that place. Certainly not after, well, you know.'

Not surprisingly, the MacPherson farmhouse had lain abandoned for close to fifteen years after its previous owner, Danny MacPherson, had murdered his entire family. His three sons he had killed with a chainsaw, his two daughters he had hacked to death with a wood-axe and his wife he had shot at point-blank range with a double-barrelled shotgun before dousing himself in petrol and setting himself alight. Even the family cat had not escaped his murderous rampage for it had been found hanging from a beam in one of the outlying barns close to its owner's cremated, smouldering remains.

'Well, it seems that someone has. Aubrey was in the other day and he said that the buyer was some English guy. Talked all sophisticated. I can't see him fitting in well around here. My guess is he'll be gone before the end of the year, maybe by the end of the month.'

'Did Aubrey say anything else? Like

what this man does for a living? Does he have any family?' Hooper was curious. They didn't get many strangers in Harvest Wood. In fact, he couldn't remember who the last one had been. Sure, they got drifters from time to time, but those folk were transitory, seen one day and gone the next. They sure as hell didn't buy property, especially places like the MacPherson farmhouse with its bad reputation.

'According to Aubrey he's a retired scientist or something. I think he said he was into plants; flowers and things. As to family, I'm pretty sure he hasn't got any. I'd say that's probably for the best, considering where he's going to be living. That ain't no place to bring up children, now is it, sheriff?'

'You're right there.' Hooper finished his beer. 'Well, I guess I'd better be leaving. I might see about paying this English guy a visit in the morning. Introduce myself and try to make him feel welcome.'

'Be sure and find out what he's up to.'

'I'll do just that. If it's flowers he's into, I can't see him being any trouble. I might see if he's got any spare roses I can bring back for you.'

'My, that'd be sweet.' Maggie smiled. 'But what would Mrs. Hooper think?'

'She needn't know.'

'Come on sheriff, in a town as small as Harvest Wood news would soon get around.'

'Maybe you're right. Besides, as I keep telling myself, I'm too old for you.' Hooper fastened up his jacket, sucked in his stomach and put on his sheriff's hat. 'Well goodnight, Maggie.' He strode for the door, left the bar and went to his parked car.

★   ★   ★

It was still raining the next morning and it was also slightly foggy with a light mist lying over the gloomy-looking fields. It had rained heavily all night and the backwater road leading out to the MacPherson place was partially flooded, making the going hard for Hooper. Driving slowly, negotiating the worst of the deep puddles, he made a left turn, the dark farmhouse outbuildings — the half-collapsed barns, the abandoned silos and the tumbledown weather-vane tower — now becoming visible on the ridge ahead, silhouetted forebodingly against the slate-grey sky. Miles and miles of neglected wheat field stretched as far as the eye could see in almost every direction, the uniformity of the landscape broken only by the dark forest of Harvest Wood — after which the town was named — barely visible to the north.

A pall of dreariness hung over everything.

Thunder rumbled in the distance and from somewhere nearer at hand could be heard the sound of crows cawing.

Hooper brought the car to a stop. He got out and stretched, staring up at the buildings, the rain pattering off his hat. The last time he had been out this way had been some two years ago when a local boy had gone missing. He had led a group of volunteers in the search, finding nothing. The boy had never been found.

Everything was dark, shadowy, grey. The wind gusted all around him blowing

the swirling mist into ghost-like formations.

On his right, twenty yards away,
Hooper could see a ghastly-looking
scarecrow made from stuffed sacking and
the sight of it caused him to shudder.
Here, there was something more than
ordinary, earthly cold. Something more
deep and intense. It was like a dampness
in his heart. He looked about him, warily,
alert. His mind was beginning to race
inside his head and blood was pounding
in his veins.

Why anyone would want to live out in
this godforsaken place, almost five miles
out of town, he had no idea. Getting back
in the car, he threw a sideways glance at
the scarecrow, ensuring that it had not
moved or disappeared, satisfying himself
that it was not sat in the backseat ready to
grab him around the throat and throttle
him with its twiggy hands. His heart rate
quickened, fearing for one moment the
sight of its torn, sack-like face with its
button eyes and ripped mouth in his
rear-view mirror.

Get a hold of yourself, sheriff, he told

himself. This wasn't like him.

It was this place though. He was sure of it. There was something about the MacPherson farmhouse that just wasn't wholesome. Evil and murder had been committed here. It was a place of madness — at least it had been, and possibly still was. The events of fifteen years ago still clung to area, blanketing it like a funeral shroud. The sooner he introduced himself to Harvest Wood's newest resident and got back into town the better.

With that thought, he drove the remaining two hundred yards up to the farmhouse. It looked very much as he remembered it; tumbledown and partly ruined, its walls in desperate need of a coat of paint. Several of the windows were smashed and in the driveway lay a large rusting farm vehicle of some description; all vicious, curved spikes and upturned plough shears. In one of the barns over to his right, he could see a much more modern looking car, no doubt belonging to the current owner. A shiver went through him. It was in that barn, fifteen

166

years ago, that he had found the incinerated remains of Danny MacPherson.

He parked up and got out, slamming his car door, hoping that he'd made just the right amount of noise to attract attention. He bent down and tied his shoelace and was just about to head up to the front door when it opened.

In the doorway was a tall, spindly, white-haired individual wearing dark sunglasses. There was the pallid look of a dead-fish's underbelly about him and his face was sunken, almost cadaverous. His narrow, pencil-thin lips were blue-black. He wore a full-length dark-brown leather apron that was covered in unsightly damp stains and he had similarly stained yellow rubber gloves on his hands. It was obvious that he suffered from albinism.

Hooper hadn't known what to expect but the sight that greeted him was certainly not it. He faltered slightly and gulped nervously. This man looked as though he had just stepped fresh from the County Morgue.

The stranger stood staring at him

through his dark glasses.

Maybe he's blind, thought Hooper. He found his voice. 'Good day. My name's Rod Hooper. I'm the local sheriff for these here parts and on behalf of the inhabitants of Harvest Wood I'd like to welcome you to our little town.' He didn't extend his hand. The last thing he wanted was to shake hands with this slime-spattered individual, besides, if he was blind, he wouldn't notice.

'Why thank you, sheriff. I'm Sebastian Rutherford.' Despite his appearance, the man's words were clipped and cultured, very English.

'I trust you're settling in alright, Mr. Rutherford?'

'Yes, yes. A few problems here and there but nothing that can't be dealt with.' The white-haired man removed his gloves and stuck them into the wide apron pockets. 'Please, I'm forgetting my manners. Would you care to come in for a cup of tea? Or perhaps a coffee?'

'Sure, I'd like that.' Hooper took off his hat and followed the other into the house. As he got closer he couldn't help but be struck by the repellent smell that came from his host. It was like rancid meat mixed with freshly chopped garlic. It bordered on the overpowering. Surreptitiously, he wafted at the foul air with his hat. What had the man been doing, he wondered — skinning squid?

The interior of the house looked as though hardly any work had been done to it since Hooper had last been here. The wallpaper was peeling from the walls and huge damp patches spread throughout. The floor was largely uncarpeted and creaked audibly as they went down a dimly-lit passage before entering the lounge. The furniture inside was crude and basic; stuffed and ripped armchairs, old tables and cabinets, out-dated ornaments on the walls and mantelpiece. He reckoned it had to be the original MacPherson stuff. He couldn't help but shiver, thinking it ghoulish that these personal effects were still here. Heavy curtains were drawn across the shuttered windows, the only light coming from a small lamp in the far corner.

'Do take a seat.' Rutherford removed

his apron and carried it into another room. He walked woodenly, yet without the stumbling carefulness of someone who was blind, leading Hooper to the conclusion that he probably could see. 'I take it you would like a cup of tea, sheriff?' he called.

'If it's no trouble, I'd rather have a coffee.'

'Very good. Just make yourself comfortable. I'll only be a few minutes.'

Hooper couldn't help but feel uneasy. Perhaps it was due to knowing what had happened here fifteen years ago or the overall sense of weirdness Rutherford exuded. He found himself staring around him, trying to establish just what kind of room he was in, but it was so damned dark and shadowy. Admittedly, it was grey and overcast outside but surely a normal person would have opened the shutters and the curtains in order to bring in more light rather than keep them drawn, and although he could see more lamps none of them were lit.

Rutherford returned with a cup of steaming coffee. 'Here's your drink.' He passed it to the sheriff and took a seat by an old dresser.

'Thanks.' Hooper took a sip, scalding his lips.

'Now then, would you care to tell me the purpose of your visit?' Divested of his apron and gloves, Rutherford now looked slightly more normal. His jacket was old-fashioned but stylish and that horrendous stench had lessened noticeably.

'I just thought I'd come out and introduce myself. You know, a bit of public relations.' Hooper rested his cup on a nearby table. 'I understand that you're a scientist and that your field of expertise, if you pardon the pun, is flowers, is that correct?'

Rutherford leapt from his chair in anger as though he had been tugged upright by invisible ropes. *'Flowers!? Flowers!* Don't take me for some lay botanist who doesn't know his *Eumycota* from his myxomycetes and oomycetes!' He was shaking all over as though someone had just passed a low electric current through him. 'I'll have nothing to do with flowers, thank you very much!

What outrageous nonsense! Whoever told you that should be strung-up from the nearest telegraph pole.'

Hooper was taken aback by the man's extreme reaction and his bizarre, unwarranted behaviour. 'Steady on, I only — '

'*I'm a mycologist!* I study fungi — the alluring, mesmeric, fascinating, biologically diverse and adaptive world of fungi. *Flowers!*' Rutherford spat the last word as though it befouled his mouth. 'What perverse lie has fed mankind the belief that fungi are repulsive, slimy, undesirable things; bulbous organisms to be shunned and feared by the ignorant? What beauty does a rose possess that cannot be bettered by that of a common basidiomycota? Have you or they ever gazed upon the wonders of a microscopic mould, awestruck by the principles of decomposition, or taken delight in the discovery of a hitherto unidentified microcellular smut, enraptured by its delicate spore-realising capabilities? Well, have you sheriff? Have you?'

The man was clearly unbalanced.

Hooper shook his head. 'No. I can't say that I have.' He straightened in his seat.

'Look, Mr. Rutherford, I apologise if I've caused you any offence. It's just that we're all a bit ignorant of things like that out here.'

'Apology accepted.' Rutherford sat down. He seemed to have regained some of his self-composure. He was no longer trembling.

The sheriff cast around for a topic that might calm the man down. 'So can you tell me what brings you out here? I mean, are you doing some kind of scientific research, writing a book, perhaps?'

'Well, seeing as you've asked, I may as well tell you. I am carrying out some rather fascinating experiments. I would tell you more, but alas I'm still at the very early phases. Indeed, I can't go ahead until I receive some laboratory equipment, which I'm hoping will arrive in the next day or two. Come to think of it, I will be needing a strong back to help me with some of the more manual tasks, so if by chance you know of anyone reliable in town who is willing to earn an honest wage, I would appreciate it.'

Hooper thought for a moment. 'There's

Butch Langford. He's always on the look-out for a bit of work and he's pretty trustworthy. And I believe he used to work here as a farmhand here back in the days before — ' He paused. 'Anyhow, if I see him I'll have a word, tell him that you're interested in taking on a hired hand.' There was something else that he wanted to ask but he was rather uncomfortable about asking it. In the end, he decided to just come right out with it. 'I understand that you bought this property from Aubrey Penton, the real estate agent in town. I don't suppose he mentioned to you anything about the history of this place, did he?'

'I take it you're referring to the murders? Yes, he did raise the subject.'

'And, you weren't put off?'

'No. Not at all. Why should I be? Those events, although indisputably tragic, happened a long time ago. Now, if you're trying to imply by the nature of your question that perhaps the house is haunted or something similar, tainted by that terrible incident, then I'm not interested. You see, I'm a man of science, not some ignorant-minded, superstitious fool. There are no such things as ghosts. Similarly, there is no such thing as the soul or spirit. Humans are but organic, biological constructs; a conglomeration of chemical elements given a rudimentary semblance of animation via electrical nerve impulses.'

Hooper was feeling more and more out of his depth. He was more used to dealing with drunken, foul-mouthed truckers, breaking up the frequent bar room brawls or apprehending teenage delinquents over acts of petty vandalism or other forms of criminality. This eccentric, toadstool-loving weirdo was something completely different. Something way beyond his expertise.

'So you see, sheriff, you needn't be concerned that I'll come running for help in the dead of night claiming that I'm being harangued by ghosts. Because they simply don't exist. Now, if there's anything else you'd like to ask I'd appreciate it if you were quick about it. I've got some fresh samples of the most peculiar saprobic myriostoma that I am currently cultivating in my makeshift laboratory downstairs and I'm sure they'll be missing me.'

'*Missing you?*' Hooper spilled some of his coffee. He wasn't sure whether he had heard right.

'Why yes. Almost certainly. I talk to them, you see. I found out long ago that communication stimulates and enhances growth. Don't look so surprised. Certain genera have been known to respond exceedingly positively to the voice of their cultivator. Although I doubt whether they derive actual nourishment from sound, it is evidently highly beneficial. My discoveries will open an entire new world regarding saprobic phenomena.'

'Right, I see.' Hooper slowly nodded his head. He didn't understand a word of what the other was on about, nor did he believe much of it. It was sheer bloody nonsense as far as he was concerned. That man was off his rocker. 'Well, thanks for the coffee. I think it's time I was going.' He got to his feet. In this darkened room he was beginning to feel like a mushroom himself — in the sense that for the past fifteen minutes or so he had been kept in the dark and fed on the proverbial.

* * *

Five days later the sun was shining and the skies were blue. Sheriff Hooper was just leaving the police station when he saw Butch Langford crossing the street. Hailing him, he waited for him to approach.

Butch was tall and well-built, good-natured but exceptionally dim-witted. He was a damn good labourer however and three days ago he had taken Rutherford up on his offer of helping him with some of his heavy work.

'Say Butch, how are you finding working for Mr. Rutherford? Are things going okay?'

'Yeah, sure are sheriff.' Butch grinned revealing a largely toothless mouth. 'I've been helping Mr. Rutherford move some of old Danny's stuff. You remember Danny, don't you?'

Hooper didn't know how to answer

that question. He doubted whether he, or anyone else in town for that matter, would ever forget Danny MacPherson. 'Sure, I remember Danny. He did some bad things up there, didn't he? Anyhow, do you think Mr. Rutherford's getting rid of the furniture?'

'I don't know about that, sheriff, but I've been clearing out the chairs and the tables, even a couple of beds from upstairs. Mr. Rutherford got me to set up these big lamps that arrived only a day or two back in several of the rooms and he's put in a new generator. You should see them, sheriff. They don't half make a funny noise when they're all powered up. *And the light!* I ain't ever seen nothing like it. I reckon they must be brighter than the floodlights they have down at Casey Park.'

Hooper gently chewed his bottom lip. 'Are these all part of that experiment he's doing?'

Butch shrugged his broad shoulders. 'How would I know? To be honest, I don't know what he's saying most of the time. I can't understand him. He's from

England, you know. That's on the other side of the state. All I do is lift and carry. He said he was waiting for some last bit of equipment and then he'll be able to start his work. I finished early the other day so he had me out looking for mushrooms. I told him that my pappy told me not to touch those things on account of some of them being deadly poisonous.'

'What did Rutherford say to that?'

'Why he just laughed and told me to wear a pair of gloves.'

'That's good advice. So, is that you done working up there now?'

'Mr. Rutherford said to call back in a couple of days. By which time he should've got whatever it was he was waiting on. I've just been to the hardware store, seeing if they sell any acid. Do you know where I can get some acid, sheriff?'

'*Acid?* What do you want acid for?'

'It's for Mr. Rutherford. He told me to buy some acid. Said something about it might being needed if anything bad were to happen. Here, have a look.' Butch reached into a pocket of his tattered dungarees and took out a slip of paper, which he handed to the sheriff. It was a shopping list of miscellaneous bits and pieces, mundane necessities and provisions for the main part. Two things at the bottom of the list stood out however — *a large carboy of industrial strength sulphuric acid and a shotgun with two boxes of shells*.

* * *

Something very peculiar was going on at the MacPherson place. Of that, Hooper had no doubt. After his conversation with Butch he had become increasingly suspicious as to just what it was Rutherford was up to. He had deliberated over whether or not to pay another visit in order to satiate his curiosity, to make up some false pretence in order to have a snoop about. In the end, he had decided to wait until Butch went up next time and to accompany him. The only snag was that Rutherford had told Butch not to arrive before sundown — an odd detail that had set off little alarm bells within

Hooper's brain. Consequently, as extra support — not that he reckoned it would be required, but if there was one thing he had learned during his years as sheriff it was always better to be safe than sorry — he would also take along his deputy, Jim Bexley.

Bexley was a thin-faced thirty year-old. A no-nonsense kind of guy who did everything by the book. His only vice was the foul-smelling cigarettes he constantly smoked.

'So when're we meeting Butch?' asked Bexley. He was sat in the front passenger seat of the patrol car playing idly with his handcuffs.

'He'll be along any minute. I told him that I'd give him a lift. I've had to make some space in the boot cause Rutherford needs a carboy of acid. He also requested a shotgun, but I'll be damned if he's going to get one. Not while I'm sheriff of this town. Hell, the guy's as crazy as a coot with a red-hot poker up its ass if you ask me.'

'What d'ya say he does again? Talks to mushrooms?' Bexley had to fight in order to contain a laugh.

'That's what he told me. Can you believe it? First time I heard him talk I didn't know what to think. He's a real oddball. I was in two minds about informing those folk at the mental unit up in Crawford.'

'I used to know a guy at school who talked to trees.'

'Ah, shut-up, would you?' Hooper had had enough of this stupidity. In the streetlight, he spotted Butch coming towards them pushing a wheelbarrow in which was the carboy. 'Here's Butch now. Why don't you get out and give him a hand instead of sitting there and talking rubbish.'

Five minutes later they were heading out towards the MacPherson place. It was dark now and in the car headlights everything seemed eerie. Hooper began to feel a tightening in his stomach and there was a cold film of sweat on his face. There was a vague throbbing at the back of his eyes and some inner voice seemed to be reaching out to him, trying to make him turn round and stay well clear. The feeling of danger kept intruding on his mind and it was only with a great deal of willpower and mental reserve that he managed to remain focused and drive carefully.

They made the turn-off and started the approach to the farmhouse.

'Say sheriff, what the hell's that light?' Bexley began unrolling his window. He stuck his head out to get a better look.

'You what?' Taking his eyes off the road, Hooper looked up and saw something so weird that he rubbed at his eyes before looking again. From numerous windows there shone a pale lilac light. There was an otherworldly quality to its strange effulgence; a certain abnormality in the way in which it bathed virtually all of the MacPherson place in its alien radiance.

'That's the light from them lamps I was telling you about, sheriff. Only it was more orangey the time I saw it,' said Butch excitedly. 'My, sure is pretty all the same.'

Hooper didn't think it was pretty. It was ghastly, eldritch. It was certainly not normal. He didn't think that Rutherford was breaking any known laws but he sure as hell wasn't going to let such outlandish activity go on in his town unchallenged. There would be some serious answering to do and if the mad scientist — as he had come to think of him — proved uncooperative then he would make life difficult for him. Hell, Rutherford had been made aware of the terrible events that had happened here. So why on earth was he exacerbating that bad memory that had plagued Harvest Wood for the past fifteen years by perpetuating the insanity? He was convinced something fiendish was going on. Why the acid? Why the shotgun?

'Are we going in there?' Bexley asked nervously.

'We sure as hell are,' replied Hooper. 'It's high time we found out just what this guy is up to.' He parked the car, got out and strode purposefully towards the front door of the farmhouse. That strange light seemed to come from everywhere and he could hear the sounds of a running generator coming from somewhere. Looking to his right, he could see that the glow was even present in the outlying barn where Danny MacPherson had taken his own life. He knocked vigorously on the door. 'Open up, Mr. Rutherford! This is Sheriff Hooper.'

For a moment or two there was no answer and he was about to knock again when the door was opened.

Rutherford looked ghastly, his pallid skin given an even more unnatural tone due to that unearthly pale lilac glow. 'Why, sheriff, I wasn't expecting you.' His words came out tremulously — like the explanation of some misdeed by a guilty schoolchild. 'I thought it was only going to be Mr. Langford.' He peered over Hooper's left shoulder. 'Ah, I see he is here and I do believe he has my acid. Excellent.'

'Yeah, but I'm afraid no shotgun.' Hooper found the light was now painful on his eyes. It made them sting and he was beginning to feel the onset of a headache. In addition, there was something about it that made him feel nauseous. Or maybe that was down to the foul reek that was prevalent once more.

'Just what the hell are you up to out here?' he asked, aware that Bexley and Butch had now joined him.

'Why, just a little experiment. I can assure you that there is nothing illegal or otherwise with what I'm doing. In fact, I would be more than happy to allow you and your friends to stay and watch. Believe me, this is groundbreaking scientific research. I've already been able to actually attune the lamp-filters to the correct settings in order to find the hotspots, to accurately pinpoint the precise locations. I knew it would have to be something outside the normal wavelength spectrum. U.V. wouldn't do it.'

'Can you talk in plain English? Just what are you on about? Hotspots? Precise locations?'

Rutherford appeared genuinely dumbfounded. 'The exact locations where the murders occurred of course. My lamps have been able to detect, with one hundred percent accuracy may I add, where each death took place. The negative residual energy from the corpse of the freshly deceased leaves an imprint that can be discovered using certain filtered chromatic light waves. It was a phenomenon I first became interested in when I read a paper on Kirlian photography. I have taken it one stage further than merely investigating the observable coronal discharges visible in moisture. By applying it to the examination of — '

'What the hell are you on about?' Hooper interrupted. He was fast losing his patience.

'I can see that you're somewhat confused, sheriff.' The mycologist pushed his dark glasses back on his face. 'Come, let me show you. Then all will be made clear.' He headed off down the corridor and into the large farmhouse kitchen.

The others followed.

The room they entered had been stripped of most of the furniture. Two large tripod-mounted lamps, like the kind used by professional photographers, had been installed in the room and Hooper had to shield his eyes so intense was the pale lilac glare that came from them.

'There! On the floor. That's one of

187

them. A patch of residual death, for lack of a better term.' Rutherford proudly pointed to a black stain on the ground. It was roughly child-shaped in outline. A dark indigo moss-like growth in which unsightly forms of fungi grew sprouted from it. 'As you can see, I've already initiated cultivation on this one like the one in the barn and I'm — '

'Just what the hell is this?' asked Hooper, looking down with distaste. That feeling of nausea grew stronger. 'Are you telling me that you've found all the places where MacPherson's victims were killed and that you're planting your bloody mushrooms there?'

'Not mushrooms or any other form of gilled *Basidiomycetes*, but otherwise yes. That's it exactly! A touch of genius, wouldn't you agree? My specially genetically-modified species certainly seem to be deriving nourishment — '

Hooper swung out and struck Rutherford with a solid right fist busting his lower lip and sending him reeling back against the sink. 'You sick son of a bitch!' He turned to his deputy. 'Cuff him and get him out of here. I don't know what charges we'll pin on him but I'm sure I'll think of something. Gross weirdness springs to mind.' He looked down with alarm at the obscene bristling moss on the floor. It seemed to have grown considerably within the space of a few minutes. 'Might be for the best if we dissolve this in acid while we're here.'

Forcibly, Bexley grabbed the stunned Rutherford, spun him around and slapped his handcuffs on him.

Hooper and Butch brought over the reinforced plastic container filled with acid.

'Okay, you mind yourself, Butch. I'll warrant this is strong stuff. Stand clear.' Hooper unscrewed the lid and took a backward step in order to withdraw from the released acrid fumes. Carefully, he then tipped the carboy, sloshing out some of the acid. Instantly, it began dissolving the black carpet of unsightly fungi that was now close to a foot in height.

The growth began screaming!

Was it just Hooper's imagination or was it trying to pull itself upright on appendages that remotely resembled legs?

'No! What are you doing?' cried Rutherford. 'You're killing it!'

'Sweet Mother of Mercy!' shouted Bexley. 'Those screams! For God's sake stop it screaming!'

Hooper was horrified but determined to finish the job. Whatever this thing on the ground was — this thing that even now seemed possessed of some kind of animal sentient awareness that made it writhe and slither in an attempt to escape — he knew it had to be destroyed. It was an unholy abomination. Something that looked vaguely like an underdeveloped hand started to emerge from the middle of the grotesque puddle. It was a monstrosity engineered by one man's madness. He kicked the carboy over and completely doused the terrible thing in acid.

Smoking and sizzling, the bulbous growths began to dissolve further. Nodules popped and burst, and nightmarish puff-balls scattered a cloud of spores. Steaming and bubbling, the black patch became more of an ooze, more liquid, like an oil slick. Suddenly the dreadful screaming sounds stopped.

'Do you think it's dead?' queried Bexley.

Shaking his head in disbelief and disgust, Hooper looked down one final time at the smouldering blob on the ground. He turned to Butch. 'Go and switch off the generator, would you? We'll get Mr. Rutherford into the car.'

'Sure thing, sheriff. I know where it is. I can do that.' Butch headed back along the passageway and out the front door.

Hooper punched Rutherford a second time. 'That's for coming to the wrong town and thinking you could start your madness here, you goddamned freak. I knew the MacPhersons and what you've done here tonight is despicable. If I have my way, you're going to be inside for a long time. Hell, there's a big patch of mould growing next to the toilet in the cell you'll be spending time in. Maybe you two could become the best of friends.'

Bexley chuckled at that.

'Come on. Let's get him into the car.

The sooner he's behind bars the better.'

The two policemen frogmarched Rutherford outside. At the car, Bexley opened the back door, pushed his prisoner's head down and forced him inside. He slammed the door closed and then got in the passenger seat. Hooper got in beside him and started the engine.

They waited a couple of minutes. The lamps remained switched on.

'What's taking Butch so long?' asked Bexley.

'You know him. He probably can't find the off switch. Either that, or — ' It was then that Hooper glanced to his right and noticed that the barn door was now hanging on shattered hinges. It was as though something immensely powerful had smashed it open. Fear was a tangible lump in his chest. 'Bexley . . . '

'What is it, sheriff?'

Suddenly Butch's blackened and dripping body came hurtling out of the darkness. It smashed off the windscreen, rebounded and fell to the ground.

Hooper and Bexley yelled in shocked surprise.

Lumbering into the lurid lilac light came a loathsome nightmare. Stomping on trunk-like legs it stood well over seven feet high, its main body formed from a thick, glistening, fungoid stem from which two stumpy fingered appendages extended. Its overall appearance was as though a man had become engulfed within the form of a giant toadstool. There was a huge gilled cap, which flopped and sagged. Oily secretions dribbled from it.

'You've got to be kidding me!' Hooper stared wide-eyed. He then did the only thing he felt he could do under the circumstances. Pushing the car into gear, he slammed his foot on the accelerator and sped straight for it.

There was a loud crumpling sound and the hideous thing fell under the wheels. Tar-like fluid splattered over the cracked windscreen. Hooper felt the car bounce and heard a horrible squelching sound as he drove over it. He was reminded of the time several years back, when he had accidentally run over two of Old Jed's piglets as he had been leaving his farm.

Then there came a terrible screaming sound and in his rear-view mirror he saw a sight that would haunt him for the rest of his days.

Getting to his feet, illuminated all too clearly in that hellish lilac aura, blackened, slime-covered, naked and with an evil glow in his eyes, clearly revelling in his fungoid rebirth, was Danny MacPherson . . .

5

VOLUME XIII

There was a good reason why the thirteenth volume was never meant to be written!

Pulling open a drawer, John Knight, forty-four, resident of Jersey and author of some repute, reached inside and took out his bottle of *Glenfiddich* twelve-year old reserve whisky. He unscrewed the cap and poured a sizeable amount into a glass. Then, with a toast to the completed manuscript on his desk, he finished the lot, welcoming the pleasant warmth in his gullet. With a slight cough, he put the glass on the desk and rested the bottle by his typewriter, the brilliant early evening sunlight shining in through his study windows.

The collection of stacked papers before him represented the best part of a year's work. It was his twelfth anthology to date, and his most ambitious; seven hundred and forty-nine pages filled with horror and dark fantasy. Writing under the pseudonym of *Edward J. Slayer* his books had attracted a cult following, much to his and his agent's surprise. All of his books were collections of short to medium-length tales filled with macabre mysteries and supernatural goings on.

For the best part of seventeen years he had lived on the north-east coast of the largest of the Channel Islands, in the parish of Trinity in a huge, rambling house that sat atop the cliffs overlooking the sea. It was a rugged, relatively isolated part of Jersey. A place that made him feel completely cut off from the rest of society, something that suited him fine, permitting him to work in peace and isolation. Not that he would have considered himself a recluse, far from it. Tonight he was hosting a dinner party with some old friends in order to celebrate the completion of his latest collection, a tradition he had observed on finishing each book.

Taking the whisky bottle, Knight refilled his glass and took a sip. He stared fixedly at the title on the uppermost sheet of paper, which read: *Volume XII — Howls in the Dark by Edward J. Slayer.* The main title came from the lead story; a lengthy, gruesome tale about a group of travellers attacked by the legendary Black Dog of nearby Bouley Bay. He didn't rate it as one of his best stories but he was confident that there was enough shock and horror contained within it to keep his avid readers content. In the morning, he would take his car into St. Helier and deliver it by hand to his agent, for he had little faith in the local postal service and besides he could do with a change of scenery.

Taking a blank sheet of paper, he inserted it into his typewriter and centre-aligned it. For a long time he stared at the empty page, thinking how to begin. This had been part of his routine having finished one story compilation — to immediately begin work on another, to leave no time for the creative brain to become distracted. He whistled quietly to himself, lost in thought, trying to come up with a suitably catchy title then typed: *Volume XIII* —

There was a loud knock at the front door.

With a brief glance at his wristwatch, he noticed it had just gone five o'clock. A little early for his guests to arrive but maybe one of them had mistaken the time. Rising from his chair, he made his way out of the study and into the dimly-lit hall, passing the dining room with its neatly laid out table on his right.

Knight opened his front door and was pleasantly surprised to find Eric Powell, his old university friend, standing there.

'Good evening, John,' greeted Powell, shaking the author by the hand. 'Good to see you. How have you been?' He was tall and bespectacled and taught history and folklore night classes at the college in St. Helier although he could have taught at any university in the United Kingdom had he so desired. A veritable mine of information, his knowledge bordering on the encyclopaedic, he had been particularly helpful in providing Knight with many tales of dark, piratical shenanigans and supposed ghostly sightings on the island, information which had formed the basis for many of his stories.

'Hello Eric. I wasn't expecting anyone till a bit later. But please, do come in. Let me take your coat.' Knight took his guest's coat, headed down the hall and hung it up in the closet.

'So, I take it that's Number Twelve all done and dusted?' Powell called out. 'I'm going to have to get a bigger bookcase at the rate you're going. And yes, I will be expecting a signed copy.'

Knight returned. '*A signed copy?* We'll have to see about that,' he laughed cheerily. 'Let's go into the study and I'll fix us both some drinks.'

Powell followed the author into the study and took a seat. 'I see you've got the good stuff,' he commented, noting the whisky the other was pouring.

'Why of course.' Knight passed the glass over. 'Cheers! To book Number Twelve!'

'To book Number Twelve!' Powell raised his glass and took a drink. 'Seeing as this one's already finished and, let's face it we all know it's going to sell like crazy, I'd have thought it would make more sense to raise a glass to the forthcoming Number Thirteen. But then again, some think that to be an unlucky number.' He threw the other a knowing look. 'Maybe you could use that as the basis for your cover story.'

'What? The number thirteen?'

'Yes, the number thirteen. The fear of which is called triskaidekaphobia.'

'Triska — What?'

'Triskaidekaphobia. It's a Greek word. *Tris* is three, *kai* is and, and *deka* is ten. It's quite a well-known fear, associated with things like Friday the Thirteenth. I thought that maybe you could work that into a story. Just a suggestion.'

Knight mulled it over for a moment. 'Something to think about anyway. I'd like to thank you for your input on the Black Dog myth. I didn't realise that there had been so many alleged sightings, even in recent years. I'd always known that it originated from the times when smugglers used to carry out their criminal activities in the old caves along the north coast, employing the legend to keep folk away but I wasn't aware that there have been similar things spotted all over the island.'

'If you look hard enough you'll find that Jersey's awash with such things. I'd go as far as to say that we've got more ghosts and evil spirits here per square mile than anywhere else I know of. It's not that surprising when one considers the chequered history of the island. As you know only too well, my library's stacked full of books on the subject.'

'Talking of which, I haven't as yet written anything supernatural regarding the Nazi occupation of the island. Now that has some potential, wouldn't you say?'

'Oh definitely.' Powell nodded to himself. 'There have been many apparitions seen in some of the old war tunnels and along by the ruined gun battery installations along the coast. Why, if memory serves me right there was even a report of a ghostly Messerschmitt one-o-nine that used to fly over St. Brelade's.'

'A ghostly Messerschmitt?' Knight chuckled. 'Whatever next?'

'Why not? After all you get ghost trains and haunted houses. I don't see why one shouldn't get a spectral aeroplane.' Powell took a sip from his whisky. 'After all, you write about phantom dogs and headless highwaymen, drowned pirates returning from their watery graves and goodness knows what else. So I don't think it's stretching the boundaries of belief too far.'

'I guess that's it in a nutshell, isn't it?'

'What do you mean?'

'Well, for all my writing on this subject, you know that I don't believe in the supernatural. Never have.' Knight turned his head in order to look out the window at the dark blue waters of the English Channel that were now glinting in the sunlight.

'Does that matter? You've managed to make quite an enviable career out of it, regardless of whether you believe in it or not. You sell books by the thousands, tens of thousands, so there must be people out there, besides myself, of course, who are prepared to part with their hard-earned cash in order to read what you write. I wish I could do it, but I lack the imagination. Everything I write has to be factual and that gets boring after a while.' Powell noticed the single page in the typewriter. 'I see you haven't got a title for the new one yet.'

'I was just about to start work on it when you arrived. Anyway, there are a few preparations I need to make before the others arrive, so feel free to take a look through the finished manuscript while I get things ready. Or if you want, why not go for a walk along the beach? It's a nice evening for it.'

* * *

By half-past seven most of the other guests had arrived. A few of them were seated in the garden making the most of the late summer sun, sipping their drinks and taking in the spectacular view. Others had gathered in the lounge where Knight was playing host, answering a few questions regarding his latest anthology as well as dropping a few hints about what his forthcoming collection might contain.

Truth be told, he wasn't that sure himself as to what it might feature. Such had been the nature of his work; always more impulsive rather than carefully thought out and planned. Still, he had certainly struck gold with his method.

'What I find hard to understand is just where do you get all of your ideas from?' asked Percy Williams, Knight's closest neighbour. 'I mean, I can understand when one writes about real events, whether historical or present-day, but to just come up with these monstrous stories all the time.'

'Monstrous? I think some of them are rather good,' joked Brian Carrington, an old university friend who lived on the opposite side of the island.

'You know what I mean.' Williams lifted one of the books from a nearby bookcase. 'Take this one for example. *Volume Three — The Drowned Dead*. What gave you the inspiration to write this?' He held up the book. On the cover was a grotesque grey-green zombie, its body festooned with seaweed, its scabrous arms extended as though reaching out to grab someone. Black seawater drooled from its mouth.

'To be perfectly honest with you the ideas just spring into my head. I know that's a bit of a lame answer but I can't explain it any other way. Sure, I have times when there's nothing there and I can sit staring at my typewriter not knowing what to write. But then, something happens. An idea forms in my mind and, well, that's it. Obviously I have Eric to thank for a lot of the actual details, you know the factual stuff and what have you.'

'Yes, Eric was just telling me that your next volume, *Volume Thirteen*, is going to be based on the number thirteen. Is that right?' enquired Carrington.

'I guess that remains to be seen,' Knight replied guardedly. 'It's an interesting premise I suppose and one that I'll bear in mind when I get round to working on it.'

Through the sale of his books he had become a wealthy man and his dinner party was the height of opulence, with an elite firm based in St. Helier responsible for the catering. Once he had been informed that the meal was ready, he made a brief announcement to his guests and ushered them into the large dining room where each took their allocated places, with the author at the head of the table.

The food, when it arrived, was extravagant. Knight lived off hastily assembled sandwiches while writing and liked to celebrate properly when he had finished each book. For this special meal he had chosen moules marinière or mulligatawny soup, followed by sole dieppoise, then medallions of beef accompanied by a generous assortment of vegetables. For dessert there were crêpes suzette with his favourite, grand marnier sauce. All were complimented by a selection of fine wines.

It was whilst the dessert was being cleared that Powell, who was seated on Knight's immediate left, did a quick count up and noticed that there were thirteen of them gathered around the table.

Knight noticed the rather strange look on his friend's face. 'Are you all right, Eric?'

'Why, yes. I just realised that there are thirteen of us at the table.'

'Well there's a coincidence for you.' Knight reached for his wine glass. 'I take it that has some symbolic meaning or other. No doubt something terribly unlucky.'

'Yes, I believe it does. It goes back to what we were talking about earlier. The origins of the fear of the number thirteen. Some believe it originates in the New Testament. The Last Supper — Judas the betrayer often viewed as being the unlucky thirteenth person there. A similar story can be ascribed to the Norse god of mischief, Loki, who was the thirteenth deity to arrive at the funeral of Baldur, whom he had a part in killing.'

'Well I certainly have nothing to fear from a stupid number. How can that harm anyone? Alright, I admit drinking thirteen whiskies might not be that beneficial, but really. It's just all primal superstitious nonsense. In fact, I've got a really good feeling about Volume Thirteen. I think it's going to be the best yet.'

'I just hope you're right.'

'Here's an idea for your next book,' called out Ray Foster, a retired dairy farmer who had known Knight for over ten years and who sometimes did odd jobs around the house. From the slur in his speech it was fairly clear that he'd had one too many glasses of wine. 'What if we were all ghosts and you didn't know it?' His embarrassed wife gave him a nudge.

'I've already done that. But thanks for the suggestion, Ray. It's in *Volume Nine* — *Uncle Theobald's Last Birthday Party*. It's one of my favourites and I'd be happy to lend you a copy.'

By around ten o'clock, the dinner party was coming to an end and the guests started to make their farewells and their good-wishes for the success of the new book. Knight waved each of them off while the caterers cleared up. Soon even they had departed.

Wine glass in hand, he entered his study.

There was a stranger — a well-built, dark-haired, angular-faced man with piercing green eyes sitting in the chair by the window. He was dressed in a long, high-collared dark coat that came down to the calf-high black boots he wore. In his hands was the completed manuscript.

Stunned surprise gave way to a strong sense of alarm within Knight. This was clearly an intruder who had waited until the guests had left, carefully picking his time before breaking in.

'Who are you and what the hell are you doing here?' demanded Knight trying not to show any signs of fear.

The man just continued to read as though he hadn't heard a word the other had said.

'Get out before I call the police.' Knight was well aware and so no doubt was the other, that it would take at least twenty minutes for the police to get out here. With that uncomfortable thought, he looked about for a suitable weapon with which to defend himself should the need arise. His eyes fell on his ornate letter-opener — seven inches of hard, pointed steel. He snatched it up.

There was no reaction from the seated figure whatsoever.

'Look mister, I don't know who you are or what you want but I'm telling you to get out of my house. I've got friends coming back soon and you'd better be gone before they get here.' The last part was pure bluff but Knight had to hope that it would scare the intruder into leaving.

Still no response. The stranger seemed close to completing his reading. But the speed at which he was doing so was unreal.

Knight was beginning to panic now. His pulse was racing and a surge of blood pounded at his temples. A knot of fear and apprehension gripped him, tightening in his stomach. He swallowed a lump in his throat and his fingers clenched around the handle of the letter-opener. 'I'm giving you one last warning.'

'Satisfactory.'

The single word sent an icy shiver through Knight. The voice that said it was evil beyond imagination.

Knight didn't know what to say, how to reply. There seemed to be something about the stranger that wasn't quite right.

He had the unsettling impression that the man was unaware of his presence. Either that or he had opted not to take any notice of him despite the fact that he was armed, admittedly only with a letter-opener but he thought things wouldn't have been any different had he been standing there with a loaded gun.

Now that the man had completed his reading he got up and returned the pile of papers to the desk. Only then did he show some semblance of awareness. He looked directly at the author; twin emerald-green slits that focused on him with a dark intensity.

'You said my work's satisfactory. Why don't you wait until it's been published so that you can then buy a copy?' Knight was deliberately trying to make light of the matter. It seemed he had little alternative but to try and befriend his uninvited guest. Even with the weapon he held, he doubted whether he could physically challenge the man.

'Why should I buy a copy of my own book?' The man's lips creased into a cold smile.

That was all Knight needed. A proper weirdo. He had read about some of the mega-famous authors in America who had been targeted by psychopathic fans and stalkers but he had never expected anything like that to happen here, on Jersey. For a while he was speechless. He took several steps back so that he was now in the doorway, ready to make a run for it if need be. 'What?' he managed to ask.

'I said, why should I buy a copy of my own book?'

'You're not right in the head, are you? That's my work, my manuscript.'

'You really think so, don't you? Then why does it have my name on it?'

'What are you talking about?'

'Why, I would've thought it would be obvious by now. I'm Edward J. Slayer and I'm the author of all of the volumes you believe to be yours.'

★　★　★

Knight woke up many times that night with the terrible images from a recurring

212

nightmare going insanely through his brain. He saw himself stood atop a cliff road overlooking a raging sea. The sky was dark and foreboding, filled with thunderous clouds, which blotted out the sun. Turning his gaze inland, all he saw was desolation. Mile upon mile of barren, post-apocalyptic wasteland interspersed with abandoned buildings and rows of telegraph poles that stretched off into the bleak, godforsaken distance. There was a figure, a dark, silent, menacing figure standing to his left and no matter where he went it followed, like a cast shadow almost, a parasitic twin. He was unable to discern any features and yet he was certain he knew who it was — or rather what it was.

And then there was the number. *Thirteen*. It seemed to have latched onto his psyche, making him see it in his mind's eye the way the after-image from a bright bulb filament becomes seared onto the retina. He couldn't get it out of his head as his irrational mind began associating it with the most mundane of things. Thirteen cards in a suit. Thirteen loaves in a baker's dozen. Nearly all office blocks had no thirteenth floor. Thirteen, unlucky for some. Thirteen letters in Edward J. Slayer . . .

At around four o'clock he decided he'd be better off staying awake so he got up, got dressed and went downstairs into the kitchen in order to make himself an early breakfast. It was whilst he was waiting for his toast that he suddenly remembered the dark-haired man, who had called himself 'Edward J. Slayer'. It was strange but he had completely forgotten all about his encounter, unable to remember exactly how it had ended. Clearly the other had decided to leave, no doubt fearing the return of some of his guests. Still, he decided to go into his study just to be sure.

The room was empty and he was somewhat relieved to notice that his manuscript was still there, complete and intact. Once he had eaten his breakfast and had a few cups of strong coffee he would get into his car and deliver the manuscript to his agent. He would spend some time in St. Helier at an early-morning café, or perhaps just take a seat in one of the parks and wait until his agent arrived at his office.

Something that shouldn't have been there caught his eye — half a dozen typed pages lying next to the typewriter. He went over. From the looks of it he must have started work on his latest anthology for that's exactly what he had here. Five pages of story, clearly done in his style. The title page read: *Volume XIII — The Beginning of the End by Edward J. Slayer.*

⋆ ⋆ ⋆

Knight arrived back at his house shortly after one o'clock. He had delivered his manuscript and his agent had been extremely pleased, informing him that the publishers were ready to go as soon as the proofs were signed off. He predicted that it was going to reach record sales and might well get into the top ten of the bestsellers list. Very good going for a book of its sort.

The author had nodded, smiled, signed

a few contracts and said little, his mind now troubled by the encounter the previous night and the nightmares that had come after. On the drive back from St. Helier, he had felt an unsettling sense of foreboding that had made him drive very slowly and cautiously. That damned number — *Thirteen* — seemed to crop up time and time again no matter where he looked. He saw it on passing buses or car registration plates. It was on road signs and front doors. On his dashboard he realised the mileage on his car stood at thirteen thousand and thirteen miles. Hell, by the time he had got out of his car it was thirteen minutes past one o'clock — the thirteenth hour of the day.

He needed a drink. After pouring himself a whisky, he went out onto his patio and stood for a few minutes gazing out at the sea. There was a feeling of eyes watching him, almost as though someone were standing close by, someone he could sense but could not see. He gave a nervous swallow, and turned full circle, looking everywhere, scanning the bushes that grew at the edges of his garden. Then his gaze was on the stretch of headland and the beach, considering for a moment the paranoid possibility that he was being spied on by someone with a pair of binoculars. There was no one in sight.

He turned and headed back for the house.

And there he was.

A man — the sharp-faced man — staring with those evilly bright and intimidating green eyes from his study window, watching his every move.

Knight recoiled in shocked surprise. For an instant, he wondered whether it was just his imagination or perhaps his own warped reflection on which it seemed uncannily superimposed. He closed his eyes and looked again. The man was still there, watching him, studying his every movement with an undeniable wickedness. This was getting crazy, he thought and this time he would call the police, have this stalker thrown off his property and hopefully locked up. He was clearly a menace and possibly a dangerous one to boot.

A sudden resolution struck the author.

He would be damned if he was going to be threatened in his own home in such a manner. Noticing a garden spade leaning against a nearby wall, he picked it up and strode purposefully back into his house. If the man would not leave of his own accord then he would be sorry. No doubt about that.

Entering his study, Knight found it empty. Warily, he looked around, checking to make sure that the enigmatic stranger was not hiding behind the curtains or anywhere else for that matter. Maybe he had doubled-back and was now hiding elsewhere in the house. That being the case, he decided to pick up the phone and call the police.

The line was dead.

Knight cursed savagely. He was now faced with two options. Either he could sit things out, his spade at hand in case the weirdo should return or he could get into his car and drive to the police station, inform them that there was a strange man prowling around his property. Common sense dictated that that was the better of the two options, certainly the safer. Reaching into his trouser pocket his heart lurched when he realised that he had misplaced his car keys.

Desperately, he tried to jog his memory, to think just where he had left them. Had he removed them from his pocket and put them on the desk in the lounge by the drinks cabinet when he had poured himself a whisky? Suddenly he couldn't think straight. It seemed as though a fog had descended, clouding his brain, confusing him. There was no doubt this troubling sensation was due to the unsettling presence of the strange man. *Hell!* Why did he persist in plaguing him?

Mustering his courage, Knight strode boldly into his study, his knuckles white around the handle of the spade he carried.

There was no one there. Nor did he find his car keys.

* * *

That night, he woke suddenly in his room with the white moonlight washing strange patterns on the floor as the curtains blew about the windows; and he thought he heard sounds below him in the room beneath, in his study. It was like the sound of feet moving quietly back and forth across the floor.

In spite of himself, he tensed and sat up, rigid and afraid. His heart was palpitating inside his chest as though he had just woken from some dreadful, half-remembered nightmare.

The sound came again as though the quiet footsteps were moving cautiously up the carpeted steps towards the landing immediately outside his door. For a long moment, he sat quite still, listening intently, scarcely daring to breathe, unable to move. Somewhere in the hall below, a clock chimed midnight; the slow, desultory strokes echoing through the big house, bringing more shivering echoes in their wake. Had he just imagined it, or had there been thirteen chimes?

The noise served to break the spell holding him rigid. For an instant, he hesitated, then swung his feet to the thick carpet, and stood up, shaking a little with the cold. Steeling himself, he walked towards the door, feeling oddly afraid. There was a fluttering sensation in his chest that he did not like. From outside his door, came the unmistakable sound of someone moving stealthily across the landing. They were firm, determined steps with nothing hesitant about them, as though the owner knew where he wanted to go and knew his way around the house with an odd familiarity. The thought started a little germ of panic screaming deep down inside his brain. With an effort, he pulled himself together. And then he was reaching for the handle of the door. But he never reached it for at that moment, the footsteps stopped directly outside. He thought he detected a faint breathing on the other side of the door, and then the handle was twisted gently, but firmly. Instinctively, he moved back, fear lancing momentarily through his brain, shivering involuntarily and stifling a scream.

Something like tiny explosions burst inside him. The door handle ceased turning, there was a pause for perhaps the length of a single heartbeat, then the sound of shuffling footsteps, moving slower now, reaching his ears, fading into the distance. He heard the footsteps heading back away down the corridor. Then, faintly, he heard them descending the stairs.

A strange compulsion came over him. Putting on his dressing gown, he flicked on the bedroom light and stepped out into the landing. There was nothing there, only the gathered midnight shadows. With steady steps, he made his way down the stairs and into his study.

His dark guest was waiting for him.

Taking his seat by the typewriter, Knight reached for his bottle of whisky, poured himself a glass and flicked off the desk lamp. Blindly, his fingers were guided to the keys. And thus he continued with his nocturnal typing, well knowing that this volume had to be created in the hours of darkness.

* * *

Three days later, at eight o'clock in the morning, there came a knock at his front door. Knight was in his dressing gown, slumped at his desk, his head resting in his arms, snoring loudly. It was only when the knocking became more frantic that he slowly began to stir. Groggily, he opened his eyes and hauled himself out of his chair.

'John! John! Are you in?' an agitated voice shouted through the letterbox.

Shambling along the corridor, a terrible hangover pounding at his temples, Knight made his way to the front door. He was unshaven, red-eyed, debauched and slovenly. His hair was wild and tangled and it hadn't been combed in days. There was a strong stink of stale booze and sweat coming from him. With some difficulty, he opened the door.

'Good God man! Are you alright?' asked Eric concernedly. Tucked under one arm he had a collection of books. 'You're not looking too good. I've tried phoning but I've been unable to get through.'

'That's 'cause the phone's not working. Besides, I've been busy, very busy,' Knight mumbled as he stared bleary eyed at his friend. 'What do you want?' His tone was surly and completely out of character.

'If you don't mind me saying John, I'd say you've been working far too hard.'

'What's it to you?' Knight snapped. 'I've got deadlines I've got to meet.'

'I don't understand.' Powell fixed his friend with a hard stare. He didn't like what he saw or what he was hearing. 'You normally take months to finish your work. Why are you running yourself into the ground like this? It's not healthy.'

Knight frowned as some semblance of civility and sobriety returned. 'I don't know. I just feel as though I've got to get this damned thirteenth volume finished. Get it out of the way. I thought at first it had something to do with the number itself, but now I'm not too sure. I'd hoped that it would have been easy to write but now it feels like an anchor around my neck, dragging me down. You wouldn't understand.'

'Maybe, maybe not. Least I can do is offer my support and advice.' Powell handed over the books he had brought with him. 'Here are some works on various supernatural happenings around the island including one or two on the Nazi war tunnels.'

Without a word of thanks, Knight took the books.

A few uncomfortable seconds passed.

Powell didn't know what to do. Normally his friend would have invited him inside, made him a coffee and the two of them would have had a leisurely chat. Now, it seemed to him that the other was purposefully keeping him at the entrance, hoping for him to soon depart. It was almost as though there was something or someone inside that he did not want him to see. That thought troubled him deeply. It was as though the two of them were now strangers even though they had been friends for years. 'Do you think it might be for the best if you were to see a doctor?' he asked finally, hesitantly.

'Why should I see a doctor?' That unfriendly tone was back in Knight's voice. 'Maybe you're the one who should see a doctor. Bothering me at this time of morning. I told you, I'm very busy. Now, I think it's time you left.' He closed the door in his friend's face.

'*John!* I'm only here to try and help! For God's sake tell me what the matter is.'

Knight bolted the door and turned his back on his visitor. Shuffling down the corridor, he threw a disparaging look at the books the other had given him before throwing them aside. He no longer had need of such rubbish. His stories were coming straight from a source far, far darker and more horrible than anything contained within their mundane pages. Unsteadily, he made his way into his study and sat down. He poured himself a large whisky, drank some and fell into a restless doze.

He had a nightmare, in which the words he had put down on paper flowed and shifted, became meaningless, gibberish. In his troubled sleep, he saw the black ink become red. Unintelligible words ran like blood down the pages and foul drawings seeped to the surface of the cursed paper like a sick haemorrhage.

Gruesome, demonic visages and bizarre cabalistic designs appeared in the margins. For this was no longer the beginning of a mere compilation of horror stories. Rather, it was a dark bible, a foul grimoire masked in such a manner as to appear as something else; an unholy tome filled with terrible teachings scribed by an agent of the demonic. He could almost grasp the purpose of the book but the dull fog that weighed on his conscious mind kept it just out of reach.

Close to three hundred typed pages were carefully stacked near the typewriter.

* * *

It was late evening and Knight stood in his garden waiting for the sun to sink on the western horizon so that he could begin work once more. High above, the sky to his left was now a darkening cobalt, merging through various hues so that the sky to his right was a vibrant midnight-indigo. Under different circumstances, the fall of this particular evening would have been breathtakingly beautiful, the kind of day's end artists and poets would die for, if they could but capture its essence in their works. The never-ending sound of the tide and the chill breeze it brought with it, broke him from his strangely tranquil thoughts.

He was looking extremely haggard, gaunt and unkempt; mentally and physically exhausted despite having slept most of the day. He had eaten next to nothing over the past three days and there was a sickly hue to his normally healthy, tanned face. His hands and fingers ached from the repetitive strain of doing so much typing and his eyes were smarting from working long hours in complete darkness. He had lost track of how many sleepless nights he had been working but it couldn't have been that many for he had been going at a breakneck pace.

To a large extent he had lost possession of his own will, having now become little more than a tool, a vessel through which the entity that went by the name of Edward J. Slayer could achieve its own hellish ends. Deep down there was a part of him that seemed to know this; a part of him that would have liked to rebel yet probably knew that resistance was futile and had come to accept defeat.

Sleep provided little succour, for his non-waking hours were plagued by terrible nightmares. The shadow-fiend known as Slayer was there wherever he went, instructing him to hurry up and finish his work. It seemed that it did have a deadline. In his visions, he now saw mindless, gibbering half-human monsters in the barren realms of his dark dreams, insane things that babbled and staggered aimlessly. And he knew that it was his book, *Volume XIII*, that was going to be the catalyst for the beginning of the end. And perhaps the worst thing was he was powerless to stop it. For when the sun went down he would start typing and at the rate he was going it wouldn't be that much longer before the book was finished.

★   ★   ★

After half a bottle of whisky, Knight had managed to fall asleep and the following morning he woke up to find the manuscript complete, the poignancy of the last two words — THE END — not lost on him. He washed and shaved for the first time in days, wrapped up the accursed manuscript went into his garage and got his extendable ladder and some other things and drove into St. Helier. At the entrance to his agent's small office he paused, catching sight of his face in the brass plaque. A thin, haunted man looked back at him, hardly recognisable. Steeling his nerves, he entered.

'Good god John! I didn't realise it was this bad!' his agent exclaimed.

'Well, here it is Tony, Volume Thirteen.' Knight put the heavy bundle on his agent's desk.

'Damn, that was quick! I'll take care of it, but you need to have a break. Leave the writing business for a while and get back to proper health. Your friend Eric called me a few days ago, said you were in trouble and he was obviously right. You've spent too long on this stuff.'

'Don't worry, I'm not going anywhere near a typewriter anymore. This one's been hell to write.'

A few minutes later, Knight left his agent's office and walked the short distance to his car. Sitting in the front seat, he began to knot the rope on the seat beside him. Occasionally looking up at the high *Jersey Welcomes Her Majesty to the Channel Islands* billboard near the harbour entrance, he quietly chanted to himself, 'Thirteen twists in a hangman's noose . . . ' As a publicity stunt, his act of outrageous suicide would be certain to boost readership tenfold . . . or so Slayer had informed him.

THE END

GUILTY AS CHARGED

Philip E. High

A self-confessed murderer recounts the events that led up to an apparently unprovoked attack; a gruesome murder scene holds nasty surprises for the investigating officers; a man makes what amounts to a deal with the devil — and pays the price; caught up in events beyond his control, a bit-part player in a wider drama has his guardian angel to thank for his survival . . . These, and other stories of the strange and un-accountable, make up this collection from author Philip E. High.

THE CLARRINGTON HERITAGE

Ardath Mayhar

When Marise Dering marries Ben Clarrington and moves into the old mansion where the rest of the Clarringtons live, she's ordered to keep out of the closed-off sections of the third floor — but is not told why. It is only later that she learns the sinister family secrets . . . but has she been told all of them? As the family members begin perishing in odd and horrifying circumstances, Marise must try to uncover all the secrets of the Clarrington heritage . . .